FATAL **SERUM**

FATAL SERUM

THE TRUTH WILL PREVAIL

SAM BLACK

NEW YORK

FATAL SERUM
THE TRUTH WILL PREVAIL

Published in New York, New York, by Morgan James Publishing. Morgan James and The Entrepreneurial Publisher are trademarks of Morgan James, LLC.
www.MorganJamesPublishing.com

The Morgan James Speakers Group can bring authors to your live event. For more information or to book an event visit The Morgan James Speakers Group at www.TheMorganJamesSpeakersGroup.com.

A **free** eBook edition is available
with the purchase of this print book.

CLEARLY PRINT YOUR NAME ABOVE IN UPPER CASE

Instructions to claim your free eBook edition:
1. Download the BitLit app for Android or iOS
2. Write your name in **UPPER CASE** on the line
3. Use the BitLit app to submit a photo
4. Download your eBook to any device

ISBN 978-1-63047-339-6 paperback
ISBN 978-1-63047-340-2 eBook
ISBN 978-1-63047-341-9 hardcover
Library of Congress Control Number:
2014943988

Cover Design by:
Rachel Lopez
www.r2cdesign.com

Interior Design by:
Bonnie Bushman
bonnie@caboodlegraphics.com

In an effort to support local communities, raise awareness and funds, Morgan James Publishing donates a percentage of all book sales for the life of each book to Habitat for Humanity Peninsula and Greater Williamsburg.

Get involved today, visit
www.MorganJamesBuilds.com

Habitat
for Humanity
Peninsula and
Greater Williamsburg
Building Partner

In memory of my mother and father, who worked very hard, but took the time to teach me the discipline to achieve my goals in life.

Table Of Contents

Prologue

Sam Abbott owns a manufacturing company which produces serums; one prevents contagious diseases; the other blocks the harmful effects of air pollution to our lungs and bronchial tubes. Drug companies throughout the world are trying to stop SAWWS Inc. because they are losing billions of dollars a year in prescriptions. Sam Abbott World Wide Serum Inc. saves thousands of lives each year.

Sam married Jennifer Snowden ten years ago in a mid-American town. They had met in Taupo, New Zealand. She was on vacation; he was on business; both were eating in the same deli. Their eyes met, sparks flew, and Lake Taupo's water temperature increased. People within five miles felt the heat. That same spark still exists.

The Abbotts have no children, only a yellow Labrador, Rocky, who Jennifer had before she met Sam. Most of Jennifer's love is directed toward Sam; whatever is left over goes to Rocky.

The Abbotts live very conservatively in an old, but refurbished, two-hundred-year-old Southern plantation home, which sits on five hundred acres forty miles from Augusta, Georgia. The home shares the property with SAWWS Inc., as well as a 5,000 foot landing strip for their corporate jet.

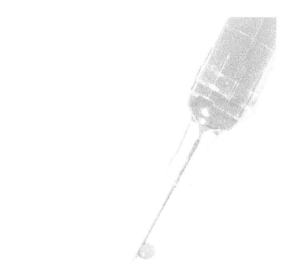

PART ONE

Chapter 1
OCTOBER

parked the Dodge Hemi in front of the house on our cobblestone, circular driveway. The sky shone blue as sea water, the air nippy. Autumn in Georgia is my favorite time of the year. I love the smell of pecan trees. When we arrive in New Zealand, we will be enjoying spring.

I flung open the door. Our bags sat in the large foyer. "Jen, I'm home. I'll put the bags in the truck." No response. She must be upstairs. I grabbed the bags and tossed them in the bed of the truck, which had a roll top mounted.

I ran back in the house. "Jen, are you ready?" No answer! "Jen!" I walked toward the large kitchen. My heart picked up the pace. "Jen, where are you?" SAWWS's laboratory is the cleanest manmade thing in the USA and Jen's kitchen is next. "Jen, Jen where are you?" My eyes searched, my throat became raw. I went to the foot of the stairs. "Jen, Jen are you up there?"

I screamed, "Jen! Jen!" I started running through the house. Panic entered the inside of my body causing my skin to chill and a numbness flowed throughout. I covered all four thousand square feet downstairs, my heart racing. She had to be here. I just-I just talked to her. "Jen!" I screamed. I listened—nothing, only the grandfather clock in the den and the pounding of my heart. Where the hell is Rocky? "Rocky. Rocky, where are you?"

I ran upstairs, three steps at a time. "Jen! Jen, we have to go. Jen, where are you?" The eight rooms were empty, except for the furniture. Everything was neatly in its place. My heart pounded harder. She has to be here. She has to be here. "Jennifer, please, Jennifer, where are you?"

I ran down the staircase three and four steps at a time, almost stumbling half way down. I headed toward the basement door. "Jennifer" My eyes burned. "Jennifer, are you down there?" No answer. I raced down the basement stairs. The basement was unfinished, dark, and held no answer. My heart stopped. I had exhausted my search.

The garage, I forgot the garage. She must be in the garage. I ran up the basement stairs, through the kitchen to the garage door, flung it open and gasped. My lungs were out of air. I couldn't breathe. "What's that smell?" My ears were burning. "Oh, my God, Rocky, Rocky, what the hell." I fell to my knees. He was stretched out on the concrete floor, blood oozing from his nose. No pulse. Rocky was Jen's second love. I searched the entire three-car garage. Jennifer was nowhere to be found.

I ran and stumbled toward one of the six security phones in the house, picked up the receiver and dialed 10, which would alert all security personnel. All I needed to do was dial the number ten and hang up. You talk to no one. My knees started shaking. Someone would be here in less than a minute. The others would be on site within an hour.

A chopper would be in the air within ten minutes. The FBI and the CIA would be calling within five minutes. I slumped into the overstuffed chair. The entire five hundred acres would be on lockdown within six minutes. No one enters or leaves until cleared by security and everything and everyone gets checked out.

I sat with my head in my sweaty hands tracing back from the time just before I left the office.

I walked out of my office at two thirty Friday afternoon. I gave my last list of important things that needed attention to my secretary, Virginia. She already had three other lists. Virginia has been with me since I started this company eight years ago. I couldn't function, nor would the company, without her.

"Gin," that's what I call her. "I need for you to pay close attention to the China Company. The one I can never pronounce."

She looked up at me and smiled, "Chineewongsee."

Chineewongsee, a large Chinese company, is trying to produce a product similar to ours. They have yet to market it. Her smile and her annunciation of the company name set me at ease. If I died tomorrow, she would be able to run SAWWS Inc.

Virginia stands six feet and has a body most women would die for. She just turned forty five last month. Her short red hair, full lips, hazel eyes, freckles sprinkled across her nose and high cheek bones give her the radiance to melt any man. Her husband was killed in a one-car accident eighteen months ago. The cause of the accident was never determined. Virginia has one married son, Kevin, who lives in Sacramento, CA.

She stood, opened her arms, and I leaned in for a hug that lasted longer than most hugs from your secretary should, unless you were having an affair with them. Not the case here. Gin and I see each other and converse more than my wife, Jennifer, and I do. Virginia will run SAWWS Inc. for twenty one days while Jennifer and I take a much-needed vacation to New Zealand.

Our eyes watered. We stared at each other for several seconds before she spoke. "Sam, you and Jen have a wonderful time. God knows, you both deserve the time away." She glanced at her diamond studded Rolex watch I had given her after completing five years of giving over 100%. "Sam, you'd better get out of here or you'll miss your plane in Atlanta."

I put my hand on her shoulder and replied, "Call me if somebody offers us anything over two hundred billion for SAWWS." I smiled.

"Give my best to Jen." Her smile was genuine.

I took the elevator up one floor to my white Dodge 1500. A Hemi engine sat under its hood. Once I started the big engine and was backing out of the parking space, I dialed Jennifer, or Jen as I call her, on my cell phone. This will be our first vacation since our honeymoon. Shame on me—I never took the time.

Jen has been the main artery to our marriage. She always keeps me pumped. She never runs out of energy. Her love runs through my veins every second of everyday. I could never manage without her.

The ramp leading outside from the parking garage is nestled between rows of Georgia pines that reach sixty feet high. From the air, the five hundred acres look like a large mansion, beautifully landscaped, with a five-thousand foot landing strip and a fifty-foot hangar. The hangar houses the corporate jet.

Jen answered on the first ring. The portable phone she held had caller ID.

"Sam, Sam, I'm so excited."

"Jen, I'm sorry I'm late." I hated being late for anything.

"We'll have plenty of time. I've double checked everything."

"Did you pack my Smith @ Wesson, 357?" My life has been threatened too many times.

"Yes, Sam. I broke it down and placed it in the black, leather bag that I bought you for Christmas last year. I also put in a box of ammo."

"Great! I'll be there in a flash."

"See ya, Sam."

"See ya!" The needle on the dash bounced on sixty. I'd be there in forty-nine seconds. I checked my Swiss watch; it was two-thirty-nine.

The plant is secured better than Fort Knox. It has two, eighteen-foot high, perimeter fences made of one-inch steel rods, with ten-inch square cement columns every four feet. Twelve, one-inch steel rods run vertically and horizontally in every cement column, which are buried eight feet in the Georgia clay. There is a twenty foot span between the two fences. It would take several days for a bulldozer to gain entrance. There are 65 security cameras taking pictures every fifteen seconds, which are monitored by forty-three, well-trained security people, who protect both the inside and outside, twenty-four seven.

The plant, located below ground, has twenty-six inches of rebar and concrete protecting its top. Below the rebar and concrete rests the employee parking garage. Below the parking garage sits the plant and offices. The plant and the offices are supplied with clean Georgia air, pumped in by three generators. In the event of a power failure, SAWWS has two back-up generators large enough to produce enough candle power to run the plant and the air generators for forty-eight hours. SAWWS is a bomb shelter, camouflaged with pecan trees, a vegetable garden and Jen's flower garden. Her flower garden is comprised of mostly orchids of every species, roses, and a vast variety of other exotic flowers, some of which I can't pronounce. The remainder is a large vegetable garden that the one-hundred-sixty-eight employees tend to and harvest each year for themselves.

The corporation has two pilots, who are on call, twenty-four seven. They are paid very well, whether they're sitting in the cockpit or in a bass boat on Oconee Lake, a few miles away. They had flown over a hundred sorties each during the Iraqi War.

Chapter 2
FIVE MINUTES LATER

My hands trembled, my eyes burned and my heart raced. I shook my head in disbelief. I just talked to her less than a minute from the time I opened the front door. "Shit!" I lifted my hands from the counter top. "I can't touch anything. They will need fingerprints." My voice echoed throughout the large, empty kitchen.

My security people will have an answer when they get here. "Where the hell are my security people?" The security phone registered the time lapse as sixty-nine seconds since I had dialed.

Five minutes passed from the time I had dialed 10. My heart was in my throat. "What the hell is wrong?" I ran to the front door, looked up in the sky and heard nothing. You could hear a chopper anywhere above the five hundred acres. The air was still. My chest felt like it would explode.

I looked at my Swiss watch. "Why hasn't the FBI or the CIA called me?" I felt nauseous. I went to the red phone in the kitchen and picked it up. A dial tone showered my right ear. I dialed 10 again. My head, working overtime, tried to piece this mystery together. She has to be on this property. You can't get out—lockdown. "My God, what have they done with her? Who are they: the Chinese, one of our drug companies, a foreign company? Shit, why didn't I get here a minute earlier?" My eyes filled with regret, fear, and hate.

Two more minutes went by and no call, no chopper, and no security. I ran to my Hemi, started the engine, laid rubber out of the driveway and looked at the sky for a chopper. I saw nothing but blue sky looking down at me.

I drove to the main entrance, the only entrance to SAWWS. I got to within three hundred feet and things became worse. The main entrance was unsecured. My throat burned; my tongue became thick and dry. I reached for my cell phone and called Gin. NO SERVICE. "What the hell? What is happening?"

My legs trembled and stiffness shot over my entire body. I managed to brake in time before running into the gate. I leaped out of the Dodge and touched the locked gate with my fingers. The gate was secure, but no one was around.

I jumped back into my Hemi and raced to the plant's main entrance. I pushed the security code to open the garage doors to the parking garage. Nothing happened. The code wouldn't open the doors. I punched it again: nothing. Security was still intact; the electric was still on; the lights on the security panel were lit. "What the hell?"

I raced back to the house. I had left the front door open. I took my cell phone from my breast pocket of my sport coat and threw the coat on a chair in the kitchen. I dialed 911. NO SERVICE. I picked up the land line. It was dead. "Hell, I'm trapped in my own multi-million dollar, sophisticated security system."

I looked at my watch. "The jet—why didn't I think about the jet?" I ran to the Hemi, slammed the gear shift into drive and screamed away toward the hangar. I have a pilot's license, but haven't flown solo in several years. The hangar doors were closed. My body was still numb. My head throbbed. Jim and Randy, the Company's two pilots, were not there. The hangar doors were locked. I reached in the glove box in the cab of the Hemi and pressed the garage door opener to the hangar, my eyes glued to the doors that weren't moving. "Shit"

I could hardly breathe. I raced back to the house and ran inside. The lights were off on the micro oven. I quickly flipped the light switch: no lights. "What the hell?" The generator, the generator was in the garage.

I opened the garage door; it was pitch black. Walking slowly toward the overhead doors, I shuffled my feet, afraid I'd step on Rocky. Reaching the overhead door, I felt the lever to unlatch the door and pulled on it. The late afternoon sunshine streamed in through the raised door. I turned and our two cars, Jen's yellow Corvette and my black 450 Mercedes, were sitting side by side.

I moved quickly toward the generator. It had a twenty horsepower, Honda engine which could generate enough electricity to run every light in the house, along with all the appliances. The gas tank, with a 6.9 capacity, was full. I had a thirty gallon reserve tank.

I pushed on the starter button and she took off, releasing some of the pressure in my head. I shut it off, not wanting to use any more of the fuel.

I needed to get Rocky buried before the sun went down. With the garage door up and the outside light shining on Rocky, I took a closer look: Rocky's eyes were still open; his mouth agape; a pool of blood had formed in front of his nose. I thought I saw something in his mouth. I spread it open and pulled out a piece of fabric. It was soaked in some sort of liquid. It smelled like ammonia. "That's the same odor I detected when I opened the garage door earlier." I ran my hands over the rest of his body, checking for any cuts or broken bones and found that his front, left shoulder had been shattered. They must have used a heavy object. Rocky weighed over one-hundred-ten pounds and would have killed anyone who brought harm to Jen.

I grabbed one of Jen's spades from the wall in the garage. Jen had all kinds of garden tools. I walked out by an old walnut tree that was straight as an arrow for fifty feet up, with a few limbs at the top shading the area.

I dug a hole four feet deep, three feet wide and five feet long. The Georgia clay made my hands sore and blistered; my back and shoulders ached. I'm not in great physical shape. Jen was always on me to work out. I tried several times, but never seemed able to fit it into my hurried schedule.

I carried Rocky to his resting place. I laid him in the hole, then ran back upstairs and grabbed some of Jen's work-out clothes to place on top of Rocky. That dog had run with her since he was a pup. I knew she would want something of hers with him. I ran back inside and grabbed a pair of scissors to cut a small lock of Rocky's hair. I'll save this to give to Jen when I find her—I will find her.

Chapter 3
THREE HOURS LATER

The numbness in my body drained my energy. I sat down in my large leather chair and tried to piece things together. My Girard Perregaux Swiss watch told me two hours and fifty nine minutes had elapsed since I had heard Jen's last words. My eyes filled with emotion; my body stiffened once again.

How could Jen and all the security people disappear within three minutes? Not possible. They must be in the plant. They have to be in the plant. The plant's generators will run for forty eight hours. There is food in the two large refrigerators. There is plenty of water. Then what? "Damn, I've got to get them out of there."

What did they do with security? Is there one, or several, security people involved? No way. They were screened. They were all spotless. I shook my foggy head. Someone should have shot somebody, or one of my security people should have been shot. No bodies, no blood. Why?

How could they get Jen out of the house in forty-nine seconds? That's impossible. Wait, maybe out the back. No, security locked that down early this morning because we would be gone. They would have locked down the front by three thirty today.

All the windows were bullet proof. The three chimneys were lined with a stainless steel firewall twelve inches in diameter. Only a midget could fit down that chimney.

I ran upstairs and looked at every window. Everything was locked down. Nothing was disturbed. I checked Jen's closet. Everything was as neat as always. "What the hell was she going to wear for the trip? Damn it, she showed me last night, wanted my approval."

My foggy head pounded with every beat of my heart. The pressure made me nauseous again. "It will come to me." I checked all the windows downstairs—nothing unusual.

I went outside; the sun was sinking in the west. I ran back into the house and got a pair of Bausch and Lomb 10x 42 binoculars. You could watch two cockroaches mate at 1000 yards with these glasses.

I went to the perimeter fence and let my binoculars take over. I walked slowly, peering through the glasses in hopes of finding something, anything that would take the hurt away. After ten minutes and covering two-hundred yards, I spotted something sticking out of the ground. It looked like a PVC pipe, maybe two inches in diameter. I focused on the object and, yes, it was a white PVC pipe. "What the hell is that for?" I continued to search the area and spotted another PVC pipe approximately one hundred feet to the left of the other one. They were the same size and both were protruding upward to the same height. I dropped my glasses from my eyes and racked my brain. I came up with nothing. My head filled quickly with thoughts of Jen being harmed. The rage in me started to control my head. I couldn't think.

I found six more PVC pipes, all approximately one hundred feet apart. All the pipes were running in a line toward the plant. "A tunnel?

Holy shit!" I ran to the house; my heart tried to leap out of my chest before I reached the front door.

Finding a flashlight in the garage, I stumbled around in the half-lit garage, pushing the button with my thumb. A beam of light struck the garage wall. I ran to the basement stairs.

I started at the rear of the basement, the same side where I had spotted the pipes outside. The walls were made of twenty-inch thick stone. I ran the beam of light from the floor to the ceiling and back and forth. I saw nothing. I beat on the stone with my fist. After twenty feet and a bruised hand, I spotted something different. It was reddish in color. I put my fingers in it then the beam of light on my fingers. It was Georgia clay, red Georgia clay. Beating on the wall with both hands, I ran my fingers around the perimeter of the stone for any sign of an opening. Nothing! "Where did the red clay come from?"

I shone the light on the floor above and nothing. "Get a candle. A candle will tell me where the air is flowing from." I tore up the basement stairs and found six candles in the buffet. Jen loved candles. I grabbed a candle lighter from the pantry and took three steps at a time until I reached the basement floor. One of the six candles dropped and broke when it struck the basement's oak, wooden steps. "Shit, I only needed one candle."

"Damn, I need some water." My throat was parched. I tore back upstairs, grabbed two bottles of water, a spade from the garage, the same spade I used to bury Rocky, and ran through the kitchen. Seeing a jar of Georgia roasted peanuts on the counter, I popped half a handful into my mouth and poured a cupful into my pants pocket.

Searching every square inch of the basement wall, I finally discovered an opening. Three large stones were lying on the floor. The hole in the wall was large enough for me to get through. I hollered, "Jennifer! Jennifer, I'm coming." I entered the tunnel.

Chapter 4

THE SAME DAY

The beam of light bounced with my every step. The tunnel was cold and damp. It would lead me to Jen. The passageway, approximately three feet wide and almost five feet high, must have been dug out many years ago, probably during the Civil War. I'm six two and weigh around two hundred; although, I'm probably ten pounds less since Jen hadn't answered me a little over six hours ago. "How did the people that kidnapped Jennifer know about the tunnel? What the hell is going on?" The red clay was hard and there weren't any spade or shovel marks that I could see.

I took several deep breaths at the PVC pipes that were used for air intake. I was at my sixth pipe when the air seemed hard to breath. I sucked in as much as I could and moved on. The air inside the tunnel burned my throat; my chest hurt. I began gasping. My head felt like it was swelling. "What the hell? I'm being poisoned." My vision blurred.

My beam of light was growing dimmer. "Damn it, I should have brought extra batteries. I came to a wall of clay. The tunnel ended. "What the hell! It can't end. No!" My heart tried to climb out of my perspiration-soaked shirt. I took the spade I had dragged along and picked away at the top of the tunnel. Every stab at the roof of the tunnel only brought fear of death. "I need to get out of this tunnel and get out now. I can hardly breathe." The clay was like concrete. After several minutes of vigorous digging, I finally broke through the Georgia clay. The outside air entered my burning lungs giving me enough energy to crawl through the small opening.

After climbing out of the tunnel, I took in several deep breaths; my lungs hurt. My soft hands were bleeding. I lay on the ground looking up at the stars and a half moon that shed some light on my dim hopes.

I marked my entrance to the tunnel with several limbs that had fallen from the many trees that stood outside the fences of SAWWS. I suddenly became disoriented. My skin became cold. I tried to shake it off. I threw up. "What the hell? Those bastards." Everything went black.

Chapter 5
TEN YEARS EARLIER

received my doctorate in Environmental Science and Infectious Diseases from the University of Southern California. California had more studies on pollution and air quality than all the other States in the union. They still couldn't keep up with the problem that began to plague them right after the gold rush in the 1800's. The problem: Pollution—People cause pollution.

I learned at a very young age, probably when I was in the fourth grade, the biggest problems our country would face weren't wars with China or Russia or some Moslem country. Our biggest problems were going to be the ability to breathe, lack of drinkable tap water, infectious diseases, and greed. True, I learned this from my parents, my parents' friends, and others. At the age of twelve, I placed greed at the top of the list because greed is what over 75% of the American population thrives on. It has been proven over and over during the last one-hundred years that greed has caused more hardship, death, destruction, riots, prison population increases, millionaires, billionaires, obesity, diabetes, attrition, bankruptcies, foreclosures, gambling losses, poverty, and lack of respect for your neighbor. I figured the last one out on my own.

At sixteen, I realized we, Americans, had abandoned what our parents and teachers had taught us years, and even decades, before. We not only had obliterated respect, we had forgotten: The Pledge of Allegiance to the Flag, how to be kind to our neighbors, the words to the Star Spangled Banner, what this country used to stand for, the constitution, not to mention the men who had given their lives, or the men who were crippled for life, to keep the ungrateful in greed mode. What about morals and love for one another? What the hell happened to: excuse me, please, and thank you?

I knew when I got my bachelor's degree I wouldn't be able to control greed or the water problem, but maybe, just maybe, I could help with the breathing problem and infectious diseases. My thesis was: Disease Control in America and the World.

Upon receiving my doctorate, I realized I wanted to improve our air quality. I conducted research and lab experiments on animals with all the passion I could muster to create something which would enable all of us to breathe cleaner air. The world was too big. It would take years to clean up the mess that had been created by greedy companies throughout the world. I had to find a way to insert something in our lungs or bronchial tubes that would enable us to inhale fresh, clean air. That meant surgery for every person. No way could that happen. I needed to come up with something else.

After two more years and lots of sleepless nights, I finally invented a serum that would help keep our lungs free of the world's pollution. Like an additive you put in your gas tank to keep the sludge from building up. It worked wonders on the animals in my lab, as well as outdoor animals. Their symptoms drastically improved within days.

They had more energy and better appetites. I went to state prisons and experimented on several inmates. Within days, their breathing improved during strenuous exercise.

Chapter 6
THE INVESTOR

Not having any resources of my own, I presented my plan to several large drug companies in the United States. I owed thousands in student loans and was almost broke. Broke, like less than $100.00 to my name. I didn't even own a car. All the greedy drug companies turned me down and laughed in my face. I hate it when the rich laugh at the poor. If I am ever a man of means, I will help the poor, as long as they are willing to help themselves.

I wrote a letter to one of our nation's richest men, David Holloway, a computer genius that gave much more money away than he kept. I heard from him three days after I had mailed my letter. Since I didn't have a phone, I had given Mr. Holloway my lab number and slept there until he called. Mr. Holloway wanted to meet with me—meet with me in Chicago. I borrowed the airfare and some extra money from my best friend, Robert Hays, from Denver. I've known Robert since grade school. He's a police officer and doesn't have shit for money, but he was the only person I could ask. He put the loan on a credit card and sent me a money order. My parents and brother didn't have squat. I hated to beg, but I needed to try and sell my idea to Holloway.

The meeting took place in Chicago at a restaurant on Navy Pier called Rios. We talked for three and half hours and I wish I could have recorded every word he spoke. The man was extremely knowledgeable and we came to the conclusion we had similar beliefs to where this great nation was headed if something wasn't done quickly.

David Holloway had a world of information that came off the top of his head, not from some printed-up documentation that was run off on a fancy copy machine.

"Sam, what I'm about to tell you is fact, not fiction, and the world needs to know what is happening, not only in our nation, but throughout the world." I was all ears, my elbows on the white, linen, tablecloth that was draped neatly over a circular, cherry table. "Sam, over 46 million people die each year from causes directly related to air pollution. Over 50 million cars are added every year to the roads in this world. Over 90% of them are running on gasoline. Sixteen out of twenty of the most polluted cities in the world are in China. It has been proven that over 25 % of California's pollution comes from Asia. Prevailing winds blow it across the Pacific Ocean. Several tons of polluted waste per day reaches the sandy beaches in California." I wanted to take notes, but he kept on talking, and I didn't want to interrupt.

Holloway loosened his tie and unbuttoned the top button on his white shirt. He sipped some water from the crystal glass and set it down, staring at the glass. His eyes focused on my eyes and he began again. "Coal-fired power plants supply two-thirds of China's energy. It takes five days to two weeks for that pollution to arrive at California's shores."

"My God, David, we need to stop this invasion." I interrupted him only because my brain couldn't seal my lips any longer.

"Sam, asthma is on the rise throughout the world. It has increased 75% in the United States since 1980. Our children won't see retirement because after breathing this polluted air, they won't live long enough." David stared out the window at Lake Michigan.

I grabbed his attention by saying, "You know the drug companies laughed at me when I presented this plan to them." I looked at the five-hundred page file I had prepared over the past several years, which took thousands of hours doing various experiments, conducting hundreds of lab tests, analyzing every aspect I could come up with and documenting it. I stared back at David; he glanced at my file and then looked into my eyes. His eyes told me he knew I had put my heart and soul into this program.

"Let me tell you, Sam, 46 percent of all Americans, which includes every man woman and child, take at least one prescription drug per day. The drug companies are the most powerful industry in our nation. The cost of insurance has spiked drastically because of drug costs, along with the amount of drug consumption. The other largest expense comes from poorly managed hospitals." My blood pressure rose with every sentence David spilled from his mouth.

"The drug companies take one dollar of every five dollars of the net profit and put it towards research. Two dollars of every five of the gross profit are earmarked for the advertising of the killer drugs they push on the public. The drug companies' profits are higher than any other industry in our country. Overall, company profits declined in the early 2000's, but the drug companies showed an increase of 35%. There are ten drug companies in the Fortune-500."

"We have to stop them," I said, my voice cracking.

"That will be very difficult in a world of greed and corruption. The FDA has over half of its key people in financial relationships with the drug companies here in the States. In other words, they own a

THE INVESTOR | 25

substantial amount of drug stock. There are more drug lobbyists in Washington than any other lobbyist group.

David glanced through my file and asked if he could review it and get back to me the day after tomorrow. I said yes and I would call him. He gave me his business card. I didn't tell him I was broke and couldn't afford lunch. I had planned to take a bus to Denver to see my parents and, hopefully, get some free food.

I shook my head in disgust and motioned for the waitress to bring the check. I paid the bill with the last fifty of what Robert had given me, stood and said, "David, how about going outside and getting some polluted air?" David gave me a quick grin; I returned a twisted mouth, shook my head and led the way toward the door.

"Sam, I believe we can and will make a difference in this nation." We shook hands. David had a limo waiting for him. He asked if he could give me a lift to which I replied, "No thanks, David. I need to think." He nodded. With my head bent down, I walked toward the bus station, rehashing what David had said and whether our plan would work, provided he can come up with the financing.

Chapter 7

OCTOBER– THE NEXT DAY

woke up with the sun shining in my eyes. My head pounded. My throat was on fire. I wiped the face of my reddish-stained watch; it read seven-ten. I tried to get up, but my throbbing head wouldn't let my body function. I reached for my last water bottle and sipped in some warm water. I reached into my pants pocket and grabbed some needed energy. I chewed on the soggy peanuts, swallowed some water and sat up. I shook my head; the cob webs wouldn't go away.

Sitting there for several minutes eating the balance of the peanuts, I managed to get to my feet. My legs were like wet straw. I could hardly walk. I glanced in every direction and didn't recognize anything. I couldn't see the security fence. "Where the hell is the fence? It was here last night." I tried to run, stumbled and fell, smashing my nose on a dead tree branch on the ground. The blood poured from my nose. I had never had a bloody nose before. I felt my nose; it was broken for sure. The pain in my nose eased the pain in my temples.

I heard a chopper. "That's my security men." I tried to get up, made it to my knees and looked up into the bright sky. The chopper was going away. "Hey, I'm over here," I screamed, waving my arms. I attempted to stand; my eyes lost focus. Everything became blurry; then went black.

I woke up again. My nose felt like it was imbedded in my forehead. The pain traveled throughout my head. My shirt was soaked in blood. My watch now showed eight-twenty four. "I've been drugged. What the hell is happening?" My stomach was on fire.

I heard voices. They were men's voices. I tried to holler, but nothing would come out; my throat was still on fire. I waited, listened and then heard dogs barking. The voices and the barking became closer. I couldn't see anyone. I tried to stand, but was too weak. I tried to holler again, but nothing came out. I saw the trees moving; the trees were coming closer. I couldn't breathe. "Jen"

Chapter 8
A FEW HOURS LATER

The time on my watch now read eleven thirty-nine. My nose still hurt; the blood on my shirt caked. My body ached—an ache I had never felt before. I raised my head, got my shoulders off the ground and sat up. I looked around. The security fence was approximately one-hundred yards away.

I stood up and stumbled in the direction of the fence. Reaching the fence, I looked straight out, to the left and then to the right. I spotted the camouflage for the plant. It was three, maybe four hundred yards to my left. "Hey! Hey, can anyone hear me?" I waited for a voice. "You dumb shit. How is anyone going to hear you?" I turned and walked to the opening to the tunnel.

"I need to get my people out of there before they die," I mumbled. I jumped down into the tunnel and hurried back to the house. I stood in front of the mirror; a pitiful sight stared back at me. I shed my smelly, bloody clothes and headed for the shower. The warm water turned cold before shutting the faucets down. After drying off, I tried to straighten my broken nose. It looked red, bent and swollen, but okay for now.

I put on a pair of old jeans and a tee shirt. I headed downstairs to get some much-needed food in me. I fixed some flap jacks that required water to mix rather than milk. "Thanks, Jen." I gobbled down six of them, along with six strips of bacon I had found in the freezer. I fixed them on the finest Westinghouse gas range money could buy. I flushed it all down with two cups of instant Folgers coffee. I hate coffee, but there wasn't anything else in the refrigerator or cupboard.

My energy came roaring back. Now, if I could just figure out what to do next. I picked up my flashlight, located some extra Size D batteries in a drawer in the kitchen and headed to the basement. I found the candles and candle lighter.

I sat on a basement step with my head in my hands. "The floor, it has to be in the floor." I jumped up and went down on my knees. Using the flashlight, I began to cover every square inch of the concrete floor that had been put in over seventy years ago. My bony knees were hurting, but I was determined to find that opening.

A half hour later I found a hole in the concrete. It was a perfect square; a square big enough for my body to get through. The hole had been camouflaged with boxes and an old table.

I grabbed the light and, sure enough, a tunnel lay below the basement. I stuck my head down the tunnel looking to see which way it went. I saw nothing, except a dark tunnel supported with Georgia clay. "Damn it, why didn't we know this tunnel existed? Somebody knew, though." I ran back upstairs, grabbed three bottles of water, shoved another set of Size D batteries in a back pack and headed to the tunnel. I grabbed the spade and fastened it to my back pack. "I better get the 357, just in case."

The somewhat bigger tunnel allowed me to run, using the flashlight to search out my path, which consisted of many twists and turns. I did not experience any problem breathing. Every step got me closer to Jen.

I reached a T in the tunnel. I had to make a decision. I took the right turn, hoping it would lead to the plant. The plant had to be closer. I could see Jen. She, she wore those purple Capri pants with a, with a white sleeveless top. On her feet were the white flats she had bought at Nordstrom's. I remembered. "Yes, I remember." I broke into a smile. My heart raced. I couldn't get there fast enough.

My beam of light got bigger with every step. "Shit, another T, now which way?" I went left; it was a gut feeling. I ran faster, faster, until the tunnel ended. My heart swelled. I searched the clay walls with my light and saw nothing. "I can't take it anymore." My eyes filled with tears. "Where are you, Jen?"

I headed back to the last T and took the other path. My mouth became parched. I ran for several hundred feet when I was confronted with yet another T. I went right and kept running.

I had to stop and get some water into my system. I slugged down a whole bottle of water, dropped it on the clay floor and ran and ran. Another T came into view. "I'll never get out of this maze." I turned left and ran even faster. The twists and turns were every twenty feet. I felt as though I were running downhill.

My flashlight picked up an object, a ladder. "Yes! Jen, I'll be right there." I grabbed the rungs of the wooden ladder and climbed till my head touched the metal door, the door to Jen and my employees. "Hey! Open up!"

I pushed on the metal door. It was secured. "Hey!" I waited for an answer. "Hey, let me in." My heart moved up in my throat. I took my spade and beat on the door. I listened. "I thought I heard voices. Hey, open this up, it's Sam." My body became numb once again. "Jen" My head was spinning. "What's wrong with me?" I cried. "I have to get out of here. I'm being poisoned again." I started to run, stumbled and fell. My legs were like hot tar; my head felt like it was going to blow off my shoulders. I tried to crawl, but my arms had lost all their strength. "I'm going to die. My God, help me." My chest heaved and I felt my hands swell up. My throat became thick. I tasted bile rising in my dry throat. Everything went black.

Chapter 9

TWENTY-SIX YEARS EARLIER – MISSISSIPPI

S terling Shear, a good looking, arrogant, young man, had just graduated from the University of Mississippi with a degree in Political Science. Shear finished in the top of his class and was bound and determined to be Mississippi's junior senator in the upcoming fall election. He had dreamt of it since he was ten.

Shear enlisted a group of college students to aid him in his march to Washington, regardless of what it took. He was a manipulator, going all the way back to grade school. He would charm the girls and sway the guys. They believed him in college. His lies were often discarded, as long as he would show remorse, which he did, but never meant it.

Shear campaigned hard against his arch rival, a longstanding, Republican Senator, who had been in office for twenty four years. Shear talked to the black people of Mississippi and promised them better jobs and better schools. The black college students on his staff stumped for him in every black neighborhood in the State. They would go into the neighborhood after Shear had given his speech, supporting him on every word he had spoken earlier.

Shear contacted the manufacturing companies in his State and told them if they hired blacks, he would get them government contracts—contracts like they had never seen before. Shear knew he had to work hard to get elected, and even more so once he got in. After a few years, his machine would be well-oiled and he would prosper as a US Senator.

Election week came and his opponent, Herbert Smith, was leading by 10% in the polls. Nervous, Shear drew up a plan, with the aid of two of his staff. Shear's campaign manager, Buddy Bracket, approached one of the black college staff members, Amos Johnson, who had mentioned a neighbor of his had been a former high school homecoming queen. Amos was always making sexual comments about this young lady, Rhonda Jones.

One day later, Shear's staff hired Rhonda Jones, a stunning, beautiful, eighteen-year-old African American, to seduce Smith. Rhonda looked twenty five and had the body of a Miss America contestant who had won the swimsuit competition.

Jones approached Smith two days before the election after Smith had had lunch with his campaign staff. It was mid-afternoon and Jones waited by Smith's Cadillac in a secluded parking lot. She wore a red, tight, mini skirt and a see-through, white blouse that showed a red lace bra, which made her soft, perfectly shaped breasts stretch its limits against her blouse. Her long legs, red, six-inch high heels, and the mini skirt could melt any man within seconds. Shear had purchased Rhonda's complete wardrobe, including her underwear. Rhonda would be paid $1000.00 cash by Shear, if she could get Smith to consent to sex. She agreed, but wanted $500.00 even if he didn't consent. Shear acceded.

"Hi, Mr. Smith, I must say, you sure have captured the voters of Mississippi again this year." She moved close to the Senator. Her heavily-scented perfume aroused the Senator. Rhonda stood over 5 feet 10 inches, and her long, shapely legs made her seem taller. Smith, also tall, and a good looking man, was married and the father of three children. Smith had been known to sew some wild oats for several years, but his affairs had never made the papers.

Rhonda inched closer, putting her hand on Smith's face. Her breasts got to within inches of Smith's chest. Smith's eyes were glued to her breasts under the red bra. His heart rate increased. He looked around quickly to see if anyone were watching. Rhonda moved in for the kill, dropped her hand to Smith's buttocks, then across his thigh to his crotch, where she found his erection. He gasped and pulled her hard against him. His lips met hers; her tongue searched for his tongue. She clenched his buttocks and he pulled hard against her warm body. Their lips were on fire. Smith had his hands on her soft, firm ass. Jones hunched him and Smith said, "Let's get out of here." They jumped into Smith's Cadillac and quickly headed toward the outskirts of town. Jones massaged Smith's erection the entire way, keeping him from gazing into the rear view mirror. Rhonda knew they were being followed by Shear's people.

They ended up at an old, abandoned warehouse. Smith slammed on the brakes of the Cadillac. "You ever do it on the hood of a Cadillac?"

"No, Mr. Smith, I sure haven't, but I sure would like to." She looked in her rear view mirror to see if Shear's people were behind them. She saw no sign of any car.

They stripped quickly and Jones bent, face first, over the caddy. Smith mounted her from behind and drove her hard against the white, painted hood.

Jones cried, "Harder! Harder! Oh, God. Harder." Smith, panting heavily, came. Rhonda looked around to see if anyone had seen them.

Smith and Jones had been followed by two members of Shear's staff. Once they arrived on the scene, they scurried up the warehouse's roof ladder. Jones and Smith were dropping their clothes when the staff, in position with two cameras ready, shot pictures of the entire love-making scene.

Jones dressed and asked the Senator to take her back to the parking lot. Smith obliged. Smith invited Rhonda to come to work for him. Rhonda smiled, but declined, saying she already had a job. Smith offered her $3000.00 per month. She quickly responded, "No thanks, Mr. Smith," and got out of his white caddy seconds after he had stopped the car.

Shear and his staff blew the lid off the encounter. The election was held and Shear got over 70% of the vote. Smith's wife, a staunch Baptist, filed for divorce the same week.

Shear spoke with Jones the day after the election. After viewing the three rolls of film from the parking lot and the warehouse, he knew he had a pro in his own backyard, right here in Mississippi. They met in Shear's hotel suite. "Miss Jones, I want to thank you for your cooperation. I would like for you to come to work for me. You will have a job as long as I'm a US Senator." Shear smiled.

"Why, thank you, Mr. Shear. I would be more than happy to work for you." She pressed her body against Shear's body.

Mrs. Herbert Smith paid Sterling Shear a million dollars for the pictures Shear's staff took of her husband and Miss Jones. Smith's wife walked out of court with a full settlement, leaving her ex-husband penniless.

Chapter 10

MARCH –
THE PREVIOUS YEAR

Sterling Shear has been a member of the United States Senate for 26 years. He is a forty-eight year old multimillionaire. Miss Jones is still his mistress, as well as his call girl when he needs someone's vote. She has put a ton of money into his bank account and her bank account contains well over three million dollars. Miss Jones, now 44, looks like a model for Vogue magazine. Her figure has remained firm and her face still has the glow that can melt any man. She works out on a regular basis with a professional trainer and has a full-time nutritionist at her beck and call. Her body is what she depends on.

The drug companies have poured thousands of dollars into Shear's Swiss bank account on a daily basis. In return, he has made sure the boys in the FDA are well-oiled with sex, money, and stock options; of course, Miss Jones tends to the head of the FDA, Mr. Howard C. Fitzpatrick III. Shear has a staff of 12 men and women to handle the drug companies' needs and wants. They work out of a private office in Arlington, Virginia.

Shear obtains inside information on drug stocks and passes it along to FDA members. They have made thousands of dollars every month. A lot of the drugs should never have been put on the market due to their harmful side affects. Some have been withdrawn in European countries, but remain on here because the FDA is reaping huge profits from the drug companies.

Shear has been married to Betty, a southern doll from Mississippi, for 24 years. She knows of her husband's dealings in the Senate and his affair with Miss Jones. However, she is more than happy with her private bank account, which never goes below $250,000. She has no idea of her husband's vast bank accounts in Switzerland. When needed, she helps with his campaign in Mississippi. She is a good speaker and has the personality to sway votes her husband has trouble getting.

Two libraries in Mississippi have his name plastered everywhere. Several streets have been named after him, a Mississippi hero for more than twenty five years, who has brought many jobs into his State. Mississippi has more black students attending college and getting degrees every year because of the programs set up for them by Shear's people. They, in turn, are given jobs in Mississippi, which brings the revenue up. He gets done what he promises his voters he can do. It took him awhile to get his machine running at full throttle, but he is now the most powerful Senator in the history of American government. His staff of 100 men and women is, by far, way ahead of anyone else in Washington, including the President. Out of the 100 staff members, twenty are black; ten of those are from Mississippi. Shear knows the game and how to play it.

On a cold, blustery, Monday morning in Washington, Senator Shear arrived in his office at 0600, as he did every weekday morning, unless out of town. Sipping on his first cup of coffee, the phone rang.

Shear had been waiting for a call from his finance manager, Howard Taylor. Taylor has been Shear's finance manager for over twenty years. He's been hiding money from the IRS for years. Shear's secretary, Rachael Smithfield, a black woman from Mississippi, was off due to a death in her family. Miss Smithfield was hired because of her color; it helps with Shear's campaign in the black communities. The call came directly to Shear's desk. "This is Shear, how the hell are you, Howard?"

"This isn't Howard, Senator. This is R.D. Mallory from Mallory, Pittman, and Herrington. We represent three of the largest drug companies in the world. I need to talk to you about some things."

"I never heard of your firm before. It's my understanding that Baker, Randolph, and Feldman still handled all the legal problems for these companies. Did they make a change?" Shear's concern shook his brain. He fidgeted with a paper clip in his right hand.

"Yes, they did, about three weeks ago." The paper clip protruded under Shear's finger nail after the "yes" came out of Mallory's mouth. Shear swore, then threw the paper clip across the room, and sucked on his injured pinky.

Shear thought he may have problems here with a new law firm. "So, what can I do for you?" Shear asked, as he tapped a pen on his solid walnut desk.

"I would like to meet with you for dinner, here, at our office in New York. We'll have a meal catered in. I realize you're on a busy schedule, but this is very urgent."

"Where, when and what time would you like for me to be there?" Sterling's pen hammered the desk.

"We are located on the top of the Marshall Building on 32nd Street in NY. We have a lot to discuss, so how about this Thursday at 6:15?"

"I will be there. Will the boys from the drug companies be there?" Shear jotted the information on a note pad.

"Yes, of course."

"See you at 6:15, Thursday."

"Okay, Senator."

Chapter 11

THURSDAY EVENING — NEW YORK CITY

Shear and Miss Jones had their love encounter on Wednesday evening, instead of their usual Thursday evening. Sterling dressed in a tailor-made, Italian, grey, three-piece suit, an imported, white, silk shirt and black Cole Hann shoes. His burgundy silk tie matched the handkerchief in his breast pocket. Shear's thick, wavy, salt and pepper hair had been styled less than an hour ago by a lesbian lady named Sandi, Shear's hairdresser for the past ten years.

Sterling's chauffer, Amos Randle, a large, black man in his thirties, rang the Senator's house bell at 3:30 P.M. Shear lived in an upscale neighborhood in Alexandria, Virginia. Shear kissed his wife goodbye and entered the black Cadillac limousine. Amos headed to Ronald Reagan Airport, where they would board a private helicopter to JFK Airport. Sterling did most of the talking; Amos either nodded or responded, "No, sir" or "Yes, sir."

Another limo waited for him as he stepped out of the helicopter. The limo driver, Pierre, a Frenchman, drove him to the Marshall Building on 32nd Street; not one word was spoken. Shear appeared to be as nervous as a married man seeing his mistress approaching him and his wife. The law firm of Mallory, Pittman, and Herrington occupied the top five floors of the 32-story Marshall Building.

Sterling Shear, with a broad grin on his face, walked into the mammoth reception area. The receptionist smiled at him and asked, "May I help you?"

"Yes, you may, Peggy." Sterling knew everyone liked to be called by their first name. "I'm Sterling Shear. I have an appointment with R.D. at 6:15. I'm a bit early, but if you could let him know I'm here, I'd greatly appreciate it." Shear forced a large, warm smile as beads of sweat trickled down his back.

"I'll call him now, Mr. Shear. I know he is expecting you."

"Thank you, Peggy." She smiled and dialed the number.

Three minutes later R.D.'s assistant came through the door. She was tall, thin, had a model's figure. Her sexy, full lips were painted red. She extended her right hand; fingernails painted red to match her lips. "Good afternoon, Senator Shear."

"Good afternoon to you too, Miss?"

"Barbra Simpson. I'm Mr. Mallory's assistant." She wore a fitted, navy skirt, with a white sweater and black heels.

"It's my pleasure to meet you Miss, or is it Mrs. Simpson?" Sterling said, impressed with her body. She must be forty, he thought.

"It's Barbra to my friends."

"Mind if I call you Barbra?" She must be five ten.

"Not at all, Mr. Shear." She smiled and turned to show her backside to Shear.

"Barbra, why don't you call me Sterling?" He was getting aroused.

"Okay, Sterling." She moved her long legs down the hallway; he watched her every move.

They entered a large room which held a long table set up for dinner for fourteen people. The bar sat off to the right, backed up to the wall. All the furniture was solid mahogany and artwork decorated the painted, dark green walls. The rich, close-weave, multi-colored carpet gave the room a warm, relaxed feeling. Four chandeliers hung from the ten foot ceiling.

The time on the digital wall clock read 5:58; Sterling and Barbra were the only two in the room. They chatted mostly about getting together later for a drink. The trickles of sweat disappeared from Shear's back.

R.D. arrived in the room at 6:07 and walked gingerly over to the Senator and extended his hand. "I really appreciate you taking the time from your busy schedule to meet with us." He never gave his name. "Everyone should be here by 6:15, unless traffic holds them up." He smiled at Barbra and said, "You have met my assistant, Senator?"

"Yes, Sir." Shear's eyes were on Barbra's. "Barbra has been very congenial, to say the least." Shear winked at Barbra.

Being so engrossed with Barbra, Shear's southern manners had slipped; he had forgotten R.D.'s last name. "It is my pleasure to meet you, Sir." What is his last name?

Cocktails lasted a half hour and all fourteen people sat down. Shear had kept his eyes and mind on Barbra the entire time.

Eight people from Mallory, Pittman, and Herrington were in attendance; five people from the three drug companies. All were dressed in suits, including the three ladies. Barbra put on a navy blazer to match her skirt and sat next to Sterling. It had been set up differently, with her at the other end of the table, but she changed it so she could be to Sterling's left. R.D. sat across the table from Shear, with his partners and their assistants scattered around the table.

Dinner was served at 7:00. The main course consisted of prime rib with garlic mashed potatoes, baby carrots, mixed salad, dinner rolls and coffee or ice tea. No dessert.

The conversations around the table included sports, politics, and the Middle East situation.

Barbra had her right hand on Sterling's thigh most of the time through dinner.

R. D. Mallory stood and spoke to the other thirteen in attendance. "Senator, you have had the opportunity to meet everyone here. We are new to the drug industry, but believe me, we have a handle on it. I will cut to the chase here and get right to the meat. The drug companies are losing millions of dollars every month because of SAWWS. I'm sure you are aware of what SAWWS has done to this industry over the past four years. SAWWS has grown tremendously in the last two years. They have a great product, but it's killing this industry. I know it's saving lives all over the world, but business is business. It has to be slowed down. What we need from you is to get a bill through the Senate that would put the squeeze on SAWWS. The President would have to okay it, but I'm told you have a great relationship with the President. We know, Senator, that you are the most powerful man in Washington. We need your help and we need it now." R.D. took a drink of water and sat down. Barbra continued to tease Sterling's upper thigh with her fingers.

Shear cleared his throat and moved Barbra's hand away from his thigh. Barbra's fingers had worked their magic; he knew if he stood, it would be embarrassing. He replied, while seated: "I'll see what we can get done. I have worked very hard and diligently for the drug companies in the USA. I will, of course, continue doing so. However, we must remember that SAWWS is a very powerful company, not only here, in America, but all over the world. SAWWS has rectified differences between our country and many other countries. They serve as a peacemaker, a diplomat, a foreign ambassador, a negotiator, and a friend among our enemies. Some of those enemies have now become our allies because of SAWWS Inc. It will, I repeat, it will be extremely difficult to get SAWWS to slow down its production."

"Senator, we understand what you are saying, but what happens when everyone keeps on living and not enough people die. We will run out of food, water, and places to live. We have to let people die. We can't keep them all alive. The world is too crowded now and growing at an alarming rate, especially the poor people in our world," R.D. said, sitting down.

"Where do you draw the line?" Shear asked, thinking of his people in Mississippi, my voters. Me!

"Senator Shear, these companies will put a billion dollars in your bank accounts, regardless of where they are, if you can get a bill passed." R.D. smiled and looked directly at Shear.

"A billion dollars is a lot of money." Sterling's eyes widened; he scratched his chin, pulled on his ear and rubbed the back of his neck. "I'll get it passed." Shear looked everyone in the eye after he had finished speaking. A billion dollars!

"Thank you, Senator Shear." Everyone shook Shear's hand and the meeting ended. Barbra and Sterling headed for her suite in uptown New York and rolled in the sack until the early morning hours.

Chapter 12

JUNE–
WASHINGTON D.C.

Sterling Shear hired the most expensive escort ladies money could buy. A billion dollars could make any man a little crazy, especially if he isn't paying any taxes on it. The drug companies were going to deposit the billion dollars into six different European banks in Switzerland, France, and Germany. The accounts would be under twenty different names, none of which would be Sterling Shears. Sterling's financial manager, Howard Taylor, organized everything.

Sterling worked harder than he ever had since becoming a US Senator. The bill he was trying to put through would be a fifty percent cutback on SAWWS Inc.'s production. The drug companies wanted SAWWS slowed down. Sterling proposed fifty percent, which allowed for some wiggle room if the Senate floor asked for something lower. He needed to convince six more Senators to swing the vote in the Senate— he thought. Sterling knew he had the President in the palm of his hand.

In order to get these six members on his side, he had to be extremely careful. They were the more honest; they couldn't be swayed by sex, money, or any other means. Honest documentation would have to be used to persuade them.

His staff assembled over one-hundred pages of information stating why SAWWS Inc. had to cut back production. The main instruments listed in his arguments were: Over population; food shortage; water shortage; not enough doctors, hospitals, nurses, and nursing aides; not enough nursing homes; insufficient staff to operate nursing homes; increased pollution; contamination from human waste; overabundance of garbage; and too many sick people who couldn't afford medication.

Other reasons included: An increase of social security and medicare benefits, along with an increase of non-tax-paying individuals. Every Senator had been given the one-hundred page document three weeks before the bill hit the floor of the Senate chamber. The drug companies were spending millions in lobbying for this bill.

Senator Shear laid out his platform to every Senator in the chamber and proceeded with his fifty-minute speech outlining why SAWWS Inc. had to cut their production by fifty percent. During his speech, Shear was counting in his head every dollar of the billion he would be getting. His palms were wet; his voice trembled at times; he swallowed three glasses of water. None of these things had happened to the Senator since his first campaign as a junior Senator. Greed spread throughout his body like a fast growing, terminal cancer.

The vote came in and Shear was not smiling. Beads of sweat were seeping from his forehead. He knew if he got this billion from the drug companies, he could get another billion from them. He knew he could be the richest man in the world in three more years. He would definitely have more than David Holloway. Shear grinned on the inside; once you get the leverage, you can get most things done and make them crawl on all fours.

The ballots were tabulated and majority leader, Senator Reading from New Hampshire, read the results: "Ladies and Gentlemen of the Senate, Senate Bill Number 1107 proposed by Senator Shear has been defeated by a narrow margin of 36 nay votes to 64 aye votes." The bill needed 2/3 of the majority to pass. There were one-hundred votes cast. The bill came up 3 votes shy of passing. Shear's body slumped in his chair as if it were full of lead. His mouth fell open, chin dropped, eyes closed, and his heart sank to his knotted stomach. "The session is adjourned," barked Senator Reading. Shear never moved. He had just suffered his worst defeat. Several colleagues stopped and murmured a few words not heard by Shear.

Shear stayed put for over thirty minutes before he rose and walked slowly out of the Senate chamber. With his hands stuffed in his pants pockets, shoulders dropped and head down, he walked slowly to his office. It was cold, with blustery winds and intermittent snow flurries during his thirty minute walk. Rhonda Jones was sitting in his office when he entered. "If there is anything I can do to please you, let me know, Sterling." Her legs were crossed, showing most of her shapely thigh.

Shear plopped down and stared at Rhonda as if she had cast the deciding vote. After several seconds, Shear spoke, "I will resubmit the bill. Three damn votes, Rhonda." Shear stood up and stuffed his hands in his pockets and stared out the window. "Three lousy votes, that's all. Three lousy votes would have made me a very rich man and you would have had five million more in your bank account." He turned and looked at Rhonda. "Damn it!" He plunked down in his chair again. "Let's go get drunk and spend the rest of the week on the boat."

Shear owned a seventy-five foot motor yacht on Lake Champlain in Burlington, Vermont. He also owned a one-hundred foot yacht in the Cayman Islands. Rhonda stood up and replied, "I'll be ready in an hour."

"I'll have Amos pick you up at," Shear peaked at his diamond Rolex, "it is half past three now, how about five sharp?"

Rhonda puckered her lips, slowly opened them, and moved her tongue across her lips. Shear started to forget the vote, but not the billion bucks.

Chapter 13
OCTOBER–
LAKE CHAMPLAIN

Senator Shear sponsored the bill for SAWWS Inc.'s cutback through the Senate two more times; it got voted down each time. The nays increased with each vote. Shear was devastated. Was he loosing his power? He had spent over ten million to get this bill through the Senate. He lost millions in drug stocks he had bought in anticipation of the bill passing. Since he hadn't cashed them in yet, his losses were only on paper. His finance manager, Howard Taylor, had begged him to sell months ago, even though he would have prospered if the bill had gone through.

Shear had helped his son, Travis, get appointed to the CIA through an unethical route a few years back. Sterling wanted Travis in the CIA to protect him in his shady dealings with the drug cartels in Columbia, South America. The Senator has been dealing in drugs for several years. He buys drugs from the drug cartels in Columbia and Mexico. His son and other corrupt members of the CIA confiscate the drugs before the sale. The Senator then sells the drugs directly to the drug dealers in the USA. Every third shipment is confiscated by Shear's people; thus, nobody becomes alarmed. Shear banks the huge profits.

The drug runners are let go after several weeks and the cartels think Shear is the smartest and most powerful man alive. The ten corrupt members of the CIA and Travis get a percentage of the money he collects every month. This money gets deposited in a Swiss bank account for Travis and the CIA members involved. No one is allowed to withdraw a nickel of the drug money from the Swiss bank until after a ten year period.

The Food and Drug Administration was founded in 1906 and has been revised several times. It is overseen by the United States Senate. They appoint the Chairman of the FDA. The FDA is responsible for the manufacturing and use of all food, dietary supplements, drugs, medical products, blood products, medical devices, vet products, and cosmetics sold in the USA. The FDA is under the Department of Health and Human Services. Their annual budget is well over 3 billion dollars per year.

Ronald Edmonds became chairman of the FDA last year. Many conservatives in the Senate were opposed to Edmonds because of some shady dealings in his home state of Arkansas. Nothing was ever proven, but Edmonds had been brought to trial three times on charges of bribery, fraud, and money laundering in Arkansas.

Several members of the FDA, including Edmonds, and a few Republican and Democrat Senators and Representatives, own huge amounts of drug stocks. Getting new drugs approved by the FDA is relatively easy. Over the past seven years, though, drug company stocks have fallen drastically, causing one hell of a stir and resulting in the selling of such stocks by members of the House, Senate and the FDA. This has cost the drug companies millions of dollars.

Senator Shear called his son, Travis, to set up a meeting on his yacht on Lake Champlain. He asked him to bring along his CIA buddies who assist in the drug trafficking. Everyone from the CIA involved in Shear's drug trafficking, except Travis, were trained to kill people no matter what the reason or who the people were. The meeting would be held on the first Saturday of October. The fall colors would be magnificent.

Shear had enough liquor, cold beer and food for the ten guys. They were informed about SAWWS Inc. With everyone seated before the party began, Shear spoke: "I will pay you guys more money for this job than you ever thought you would ever see in a lifetime. You will each get ten million dollars, but you won't be able to touch it for ten years." Every ear in the galley was tuned to the Senator. Travis's mouth hung open.

He told them he wanted the plant destroyed and its entire work force killed. He wanted it to look like Sam Abbott, or a terrorist attack, had killed them. He wanted SAWWS Inc.'s bank account closed. He wanted Sam Abbott's bank account closed, all communication systems taken out, his wife beaten and then drowned in Oconee Lake. Shear, perspiring, continued: "I want Sam Abbott killed." Shear paused, thinking of the millions he'd have. I'll be the richest man in the world. "I need this all done on October 12th next year. I have learned from very good sources that the land sits on top of tunnels that were used during the Civil War. You have one year, plus a few days, to get this mission accomplished."

Shear informed them before he left and they began eating and drinking: "SAWWS Inc. is like Fort Knox. Even with the tunnels, this will be a very difficult job. Any mistakes of any kind will cost you and me. On October 15th, the ten million will be put into your Swiss bank accounts. Good luck to all of you. Remember, not a word is to be spoken to me or to anyone else. My son, Travis, will be the only person talking to me about this plan. You men converse with him, only. If there aren't any questions, then the boat is yours for the night."

Shear had invited ten gorgeous ladies to arrive at the boat after three hours of eating and drinking. He headed to the airport and flew back to D.C. to attend a dinner party with his wife and several close friends from the Senate. He knew he would get the billion dollars, no matter what the cost.

The CIA had been involved in several scandalous encounters since its inception in 1947. FDR formed the CIA to spy against enemy countries of the United States, predominantly communist countries. They were later used in the Korean War to spy against North Korea. The CIA organized the Bay of Pigs with Cuba in the late fifties, which turned into a fiasco and drew many questions from Americans; the answers were never disclosed. According to news articles printed during the Vietnam War, the Phoenix Program, when more than 20,000 Vietnamese were slaughtered, was another CIA initiative. Secrets were kept inside the forty-six million dollar building that sits on the Potomac River. In the 50s the CIA used LSD, or d-lysergic acid diethylamide 25, to control the human brain. They could erase or alter the mind. These experiments were conducted in U.S. prisons and mental institutions. The outcome of LSD on our American streets triggered fried brains and hundreds dying.

During the Vietnam War, it had been reported Air America, a CIA service, had hauled in arms and ammunition while taking out crack cocaine stuffed in the body bags of dead soldiers. This cocaine got dispersed on the streets of many large cities in America. Several articles were printed accusing the CIA of assassinating JFK, but it was never proven. It was believed that JFK had tried to shut down the CIA prior to his death.

Other articles spoke of the CIA as being precious; it couldn't be entrusted to the American people. Moral restraint had a very low priority inside the Company.

During the 90s, the CIA entered sleep mode. Some people said that's when they are working the hardest. Others believed it was due to the budget cuts imposed by the administration. After the turn of the century, the CIA informed The White House there were weapons of mass destruction in Iraq. When 9/11 killed over 3000 men and women in New York City, fingers were pointed at the CIA. The CIA insisted it had proof Iraq was buying uranium from Africa. Then the war began, and thousands died, not to mention the tens of thousands who were maimed, both physically and mentally.

No one knows outside its walls how many the CIA employees. The CIA budget for 2009 exceeded 30 billion dollars. Questions get asked, but it is never revealed where the money is spent.

Any covert action by the CIA must be approved by the President. The CIA's primary duty is to gather information on US enemies, terrorists, drug smugglers, or anything else which may cause harm to the United States.

Chapter 14

FATHER AND SON

Travis called his father on the 2nd of April following the October meeting. "Shear speaking."

"Father, this is Travis. I need to talk to you soon." Sterling felt his voice seemed hurried.

"Okay! How about meeting at the yacht on the lake?" Shear checked his calendar. "How about Thursday morning, say about 11:30?"

"I'll be there." The phone went dead. Sterling's armpits felt sweaty. Shear pondered, with his hands holding his face and his elbows on the solid mahogany desk. The people dying didn't bother Shear. The risk his son would be taking didn't bother him. The billion dollars that hadn't reached his bank account yet worried him.

Shear didn't give a damn about the people of Mississippi, as long as he got their votes. He could care less about his wife, unless he needed her to campaign on his behalf or help entertain friends or colleagues from the Senate. Rhonda was his mistress, slut, whore and money maker. He could care less about her, as well. He could easily find another bitch to screw. Another bitch to make him money, yeah! Rhonda's getting old anyway.

Thursday morning at 11:25 Sterling arrived at his yacht on Lake Champlain. His son, Travis, stood on the dock, hands in his suit pants. He squinted from the sun as his father approached him. "Morning, Travis. It sure is a very beautiful morning." Sterling, whistling, walked toward his son at a good clip.

"Hello, Father." Travis followed his father onto the boat and into the main cabin.

"So, what's on your mind?"

"We have found the Civil War tunnels that lead directly to the plant. I can't believe when they built the plant they didn't see them. They were within a few feet of them. The house has a tunnel right under it that we can use to take Abbott's wife out. Anyway, we can use the tunnels to lead them out of the plant and then gas them while they're in the tunnel. We'll capture Abbott's wife seconds before Abbott, himself, gets to the house. You won't believe this father: The Abbotts are going to New Zealand on the 12th of October. They booked this trip three weeks ago. How did you pick the date?"

Shear smiled, scratched his chin and replied, "The drug companies gave me until October 30th to shut SAWWS down."

"Wow! It sure worked out great. We'll have to time it just right. Our only hitch is the gas we will use. It's a new product our labs in Kenya have developed. It will kill you in a matter of minutes, but some people can be immune to it. The percentage is very low, like less than .2%. They have used it in Kenya for several years to curb their population. This gas works better than AIDS." Travis grinned. "The people in the tunnel will die, anyway, from lack of oxygen."

"We can access SAWWS' bank accounts real easy. The money will be transferred to the underground account in the Caymans. Abbott and his wife have three checking accounts and three saving accounts. We can access those quickly, as well. We will deposit their money into a Swiss account named, "Tunnel One." His credit cards will be stopped on October 12th at ZERO HOUR, the time of his wife's capture. The electric will be turned off at precisely the same time Abbott leaves the office. We will shut down the phone lines seconds after he enters the home." Sterling showed a shit-eating grin from ear to ear while playing with his Rolex.

"Abbott's cell phone and his wife's cell phone will be disconnected within seconds after he walks into his home. He has three emergency phones in the house that send a message to security, the FBI, and the CIA. They will be shut down an hour before ZERO HOUR. Security people will all be destroyed one hour before ZERO HOUR, except those in the plant. They have, maybe, three inside the plant at any given time.

"His hangar for the jet will be locked down and its starter switch dismantled. Abbott knows how to fly. SAWWS' two pilots will be executed on the morning of the 12th and dumped in Oconee Lake. They won't come up.

"Abbott's wife will be executed by cutting her throat. She'll also have her teeth knocked out and her fingers cut off. She'll eventually float to the top of Oconee Lake. It will take weeks to identify her." Travis grabbed a cold Heineken from the refrigerator. He twisted off the cap and slugged half of it down. "Everything we do will look as though Muslim extremists are responsible." Travis swallowed more beer.

"The Muslims severely mistreat their women." Sterling smiled.

"I believe you have everything under control. What about Abbott? How do you take care of Abbott?" Sterling grabbed a bottle of Jamison Irish Whiskey and poured himself a triple shot over three ice cubes, in a crystal glass. He put the glass to his lips and drank half of it in two swallows.

Travis slugged the remainder of his Heineken down and grabbed another one. "We'll let him live for two or three days; then, hope he finds the tunnels. He'll be gassed in the tunnel. He can't get out of the complex without tunneling. The gates will be locked down with no electric source to open them. If Abbott lives, more than likely he will head for his brother's place in Atlanta. We will kill Randy, Abbott's brother, and make sure that the police in Atlanta see enough evidence to incriminate Sam Abbott. We will work with the FBI and make them believe Sam Abbott went berserk and killed all of his people, or the Muslims committed the crime."

"What about Randy Abbott? Isn't that a friend of yours?" Sterling shot a half-grin at his son.

"Yes, father, but ten million can buy me another friend." Travis had a big grin on his face.

"What if someone lives? What can they do?" Shear asked, with a twisted grin on his confident face.

"I guess nothing, but it would be better if no one survived." Travis gulped the last of his second beer.

"No one is to be left alive. I don't want any loose ends. Do you understand? I don't want any questions unanswered. I want you to make sure, damn sure, that everyone is dead. Do you understand me, son?"

"Yes, father." Travis grabbed another beer from the refrigerator.

"I'm heading back. Your mother and I are going out to dinner tonight. She said it was something important. She's buying." Sterling grinned like he knew what it was about.

"We will handle it father, don't worry, and tell mother I said hi."

Chapter 15

OCTOBER—
24 HOURS LATER

woke up with my face laying in my vomit. The time: 2: 29. It has been twenty four hours since I talked to Jen. My head hurt and my body lay limp.

I tried to move, but the muscles in my body seemed frozen. My skin seemed cold. I breathed slowly, afraid to inhale more poison. I inhaled faster, making my body twitch. I moved very slowly until I was able to sit up. I shook my head trying to rid the pain that lingered above my eyes. I massaged my temples and took in deep breaths. A few minutes later, I rose from where I thought I had died and followed my instincts back to the house.

I reached the basement of my house and climbed out of the tunnel that had almost become my grave. Lying on the basement floor, I sobbed and began to pray. Something I hadn't done since my childhood grade school days. I believed all my people had perished in the toxic gases. I thought of Gin, then the others. How they had given their all to SAWWS for all these years. "Why? Why are you doing this to me? Who are you?"

I managed to pick myself up off the floor and climb the wooden stairs. I collapsed in my leather chair. My heart ached with the losses.

I heard the roar of a chopper and glanced at my watch. I must have dozed off. Four hours had elapsed since I had sat in my chair. I ran to the window and looked up through the Georgia pines and spotted two OH-58D Kiowa warrior helicopters. They have two seats, a single engine and laser capabilities. My brother, Randy, had flown them in Afghanistan. I ran to the bathroom located in the center of the house. The choppers circled the 500 acres several times. My heart swelled again. I don't trust anyone. The noise faded.

I had to get out. I could neither drive nor fly. Even if I could, they would spot me for sure. I had to dig my way out. The existing tunnels are not safe. It will take me days to dig out of here. I looked at my blistered hands. My body ached. Thoughts of Jen raced through my throbbing head. Those thoughts tightly swelled my chest. I ran to the front door and sucked in some Georgia air. The tears ran down my cheeks. I dropped to my knees and prayed again.

I had to have a game plan. First thing, make a list of all the edible food left in the house. My heart sank to my knees. I had, maybe, enough to last three days, if I stretched it. My decision was already determined for me. The thought of using the existing tunnel made my throat tighten. I swallowed, trying to take the tightness away. I did not have enough food or energy to dig a new tunnel. I had no choice but to use the existing tunnel. I sucked in some more fresh, Georgia air.

A minute later I walked to the window in the den and looked past the two security fences. I captured a visual of Jen waving at me. My eyes watered. I rubbed my wet eyes with the backs of my thumbs. I grabbed the binoculars and stared out the window to the first PVC pipe sticking out of the ground. Thoughts churned in my head. What would I do when I escaped? Would Randy's place be safe? Would he be put in danger? How would I get to his place? How would I get to anyplace? I don't have much cash. Five hundred dollars is all. If I used a credit card, they, whoever they are, could trace me in a day. I can't write a check, either. I might have to steal a car. No, then everyone would be chasing me. Maybe they are all chasing me now. I turned from the window. My heart filled with fear. I had to disguise myself. Jen occasionally used highlighter on her hair. I would let my beard grow out.

I went to the bathroom off the kitchen and peered at a startled, wealthy man, who was running from fear and wanted so desperately to find his wife—find her alive. "God, how could this happen? Help me, God." I sobbed; then threw cold water on my face. If only I had arrived ten minutes sooner, Jen and I would be in New Zealand. I slammed my fist at the wall. My hand had been aching; now, it hurt like hell. I looked at it and flexed my wrist. Bending my fingers, I realized nothing seemed broken. The swelling and redness, however, had begun.

Randy lived in Atlanta. Randy had a former college roommate with the CIA. I need a friend. "Do I have any friends?" I reached for the phone, but the line remained dead. My cell's dead, dead like concrete. "Wait, where is Jen's cell phone?" I ran outside to the Hemi and grabbed everything I had put in the bed of the truck. I opened everything up; her phone was nowhere to be found. It must be in her purse. I searched everywhere. No purse—gone, like everyone else.

I grabbed the same spade I had used to bury Rocky and headed back to the tunnel. Before entering the tunnel, I turned and ran upstairs to get a dish cloth from the kitchen drawer. I soaked it with water and put it around my neck. I would use the towel to cover my nose and mouth to prevent, or at least slow, the poison from entering my lungs again. I would dig an exit hole right next to the first PVC pipe protruding out of the ground.

I located the first PVC pipe with my trusty flashlight. I stood the light on the floor; it shone on my escape route. I began to dig and thoughts of the awful poison smell trickled into my head. I shook my head and dug faster. When the spade slammed through the Georgia topsoil, my heart opened up like a new baby chick popping out of an egg. I only wanted a small opening until my escape, which I figured wouldn't be until after dark. I headed back to the house with promise in my heart.

Chapter 16

THREE YEARS AGO – MACON, GEORGIA

C heryl Roberta Hanley graduated from Cochran High School in Bleckley County, Georgia. Cheryl had wanted to become a massage therapist since the eighth grade. Her Aunt Ruby, her mother's sister, worked very hard in a pecan processing plant south of Macon. Ruby cared for Cheryl because her sister, Cheryl's mother, Pearl, was a lewd woman, an alcoholic, and a delinquent trailer renter, who lived in South Macon. Cheryl would give her Aunt neck and shoulder massages every night after Ruby came home from work. Her Aunt swore her niece had magic fingers, even at the age of thirteen. She repeatedly encouraged her to become a massage therapist.

Cheryl started massage school in Macon the summer after graduation. Her Aunt financed her schooling and Cheryl stayed with her Uncle Freddy Snodgrass. Freddy was her mother's brother. Cheryl's father, Wilber Hanley, had died while serving in the Marines at the age of thirty-eight; Cheryl was sixteen. Pearl had begun drinking and sleeping around at that time. Pearl had been a good looking, well proportioned woman in her thirties. Her father, a star athlete in three sports in high school, had full-ride scholarships to five colleges in the southeastern conference, but opted to go into the Marines right out of high school. He lay dying in the jungle of Columbia, South America, for days before his body was discovered. Several Marines had carried him out in a helicopter. He died on the way to the military hospital on a navy ship. The bullets that had killed him were from guns only the CIA were allowed to have. The reports trickled out from the CIA's office months later about Wilbur Hanley being involved in drug operations with the Columbian cartels. Hanley became another dead person who couldn't defend himself from the truth.

Cheryl graduated in the top of her class in January. She worked for "The Touch of Class Health Spa" for two years. Working very hard and capturing her own clientele, she had earned enough money to open her own spa. "Magic Fingers Massage Spa" became an overnight success. Her customers followed her to her new spa, which was on the up and up. Her clients were a mix of men and women, most of whom were upper class citizens of the Macon area. Cheryl's personality, empathy for her clients, integrity, and desire to be the best, made her a success—not to mention her magic fingers.

Three years later, on a cold, wet, March afternoon around the five o'clock closing time, the bell on the front door of her shop rang as Cheryl was cleaning up her rooms. Cheryl turned around and walked toward the front door. There stood Herby Woody Saunders. Herby had been the Democratic Chairman for the State of Georgia for several years, but hadn't held that position for several years, mainly due to his social life, especially with other women. Short, fat, bald, with a nose knurled like volcanic rock, he was one of the State's wealthiest citizens. He had inherited most of his money from his father, who had been a large land developer in Macon. He continued to add to his wealth, in large part, by illegal means. One thing for certain, Herby Woody Saunders never did any physical work, let alone any work to speak of, during his entire lifetime. Herby had married four times and had beaten at least three of his former wives, but had never been prosecuted because they were paid off, or so the rumors ran.

"Hi, may I help you?" Cheryl said, with a friendly smile, not knowing who she was speaking to.

"You bet you can, sweetheart!" His eyes danced all over Cheryl's tall, slender body, as if she were for sale. "I want a massage." His hand reached down to his crotch and pawed his privates as if they were precious stones.

Cheryl flushed immediately. She had never feared anyone since getting into the business. However, she quickly became frightened of Herby. His eyes were telling her he wanted more than a massage. "When would you like an appointment?" Cheryl moved quickly toward her counter and opened the appointment book.

"Right now, honey!" He grabbed at his crotch again.

Cheryl's mouth became dry and her heart hammered before she spoke. "This place is on the up and up. I think you may be looking for something else." Cheryl's eyes fixed dead on Herby's eyes.

I got a hundred dollars right here." He pulled a wad of money out of his front pants pocket. "Tuck this in your cleavage, sweetie, and let's get on with it."

"I'm closed and you need to leave now, or I will call the police." Cheryl spoke fast, but her mouth stayed dry as old straw in a barn.

"You refusing me, honey?" He walked toward her. Cheryl picked up the phone and dialed 911. "Put that damn phone down or I'll have you closed down before you can blink."

"Get out!" She pointed toward the door. "I run a legitimate business here. I don't cater to your kind." Cheryl put the phone down with a crash.

Herby's face flushed. He marched toward the door, flung it open, turned, and said, "I will see to it that you are closed down and you will never have another business in this State." His pudgy mouth spit a stream of saliva with every word.

Cheryl locked the door and sat in the waiting area, crying.

Chapter 17
THE ESCAPE

gathered everything I thought I would need to survive once I got outside the fence of SAWWS Inc. I took a warm shower with the aide of the Honda generator and put on a pair of Calvin Klein jeans, a navy Izod pullover polo shirt and a pair of Nike tennis shoes. I carefully repacked the suitcase as Jennifer had it and placed the suitcase back in the Hemi, leaving the keys in the ignition. I made sure the house remained just as Jennifer had left it. I grabbed a new toothbrush, tooth paste and stick deodorant and shoved them into a backpack, along with two changes of underwear. I added two more Izod shirts from the closet and another pair of old Wrangler jeans. The backpack also contained a can of peaches, a can opener, spoon and three bottles of water, my 357 and two boxes of ammo. I dyed my hair blond. Looking in the mirror again, I didn't recognize my face. I hadn't shaved since all hell had hit SAWWS. My malnourished body looked old and sick. My nose bent to my left.

Before leaving, I double checked everything to make sure nothing looked out of order. I don't know why, but I wanted to make sure whoever came after me would figure I was lying dead somewhere in the poisoned tunnel.

I headed toward the basement stairs and realized I should wedge the basement door from the basement side to hold off anyone who might be on my tail. I had seen that several times in old westerns I used to watch as a child. I ran to the garage, dropping my backpack on the kitchen floor. In the garage, I found two cedar 2 X 10's, twelve feet long. Jen was going to use them to build a mulching pit when we returned from New Zealand.

I grabbed a Stanley, 20-foot tape measure from the drawer in the garage and headed for the basement to measure from the wall facing the staircase to the basement door.

Running back to the garage, I took the hand saw off the wall and measured the two cedar 2 X 10's. Cutting several inches off each board, I carried them to the basement stairs. After shutting the basement door, I wedged the one board and it fit snuggly. I sighed, took the board back down, laid it on the stairs and returned to the garage to clean up the saw dust and hang the saw back where it belonged. I returned the measuring tape to the drawer.

The time on my watch read 5:48 P.M. The sun would be setting shortly and I wanted to be out and on the run at nightfall. I checked the sun in the west; it gave me maybe thirty minutes before it would be down. I had an hour; my freedom would lead me to Jennifer. I sat down in my leather chair, with my backpack on the floor next to my feet. I laid my head back and said a quick prayer when I thought I heard the sound of a helicopter.

I ran to the window and glanced up into the sky. Several paratroopers were floating toward the front yard. Gasping, I grabbed my backpack and headed down the basement stairs. Thanks, again, Jen for getting these boards. I wedged them against the two-inch thick door and the internal wall. The wedge would give me some time, I hoped. I heard voices and feet pounding on the floor above.

I ran as fast as I could through the tunnel. I reached my destination and began to dig a hole above my head. I saw daylight facing me.

I didn't spot anyone around the house. I had to wait. No way could I chance leaving before dark. I lay there, thinking of Jen. The warmth of her body touching mine made my loins heat up. "I'll find you, Jen. I'm so sorry I didn't get here sooner." Hardness formed in my stomach.

An hour later, the night air covered Southeastern Georgia. I stuck the shovel up the hole and opened the freedom hole wider. I wanted out and dug into the red clay with everything I had, until I could wedge my head through the hole. I listened for any sounds. Dead silence filled my ears. I fell back into the hole and dug some more until my bruised and tired shoulders squeezed through the hole. I WAS FREE. I WAS OUT. I ran. My legs were weak, but I kept on running. I knew there was a creek to the west, maybe two miles. I wanted to jump into that creek and soak up my freedom.

Chapter 18

OCTOBER 14th – TWIGGS COUNTY, GEORGIA

C heryl had moved her shop several months ago to Twiggs County, just south of Macon, two miles off of Highway 23. She rented a small, two bedroom house, with lots of trees and flowers. Her home sat secluded and, hopefully, away from Herby Saunders. Some of her clients helped with the move. She kept the same name for her business. Her clients followed her the extra thirty miles. Cheryl never advertised, as she didn't want Mr. Saunders coming anywhere near her house. She still had horrid memories of that afternoon.

It was on a Thursday, around 4:30; Cheryl had given five, one-hour massages and felt tired. She had been in the house for two months and her business increased every week. Cheryl turned the open sign to closed, shut the door and locked it.

Cheryl trimmed her hair with a pair of scissors before taking a hot shower and washing her long, brown hair. She stood naked in front of the mirror, still cutting her hair. She never heard the noise.

The bathroom door was closed, but not locked. The door hung behind her, as she continued to snip away. Her eyes remained focused on her hair when the bathroom door flew open, banging against the wall. A startled look came over her as she saw Herby Saunders' image in the mirror. He stood in the doorway with a big grin on his sweaty, pudgy face.

Cheryl spun around grabbing the scissors off the vanity and screamed, "Get the hell out of here, or you will die." She clenched the scissors in her right hand, holding them high above her head.

Herby pulled five hundred dollars from his pants pocket and stuck it in her face. With a grin, he moved toward Cheryl. "I'm gonna make you squeal." Cheryl backed up against the sink, her eyes as big as saucers, her mouth sucking in Herby's foul breath. Her hand with the scissors wasn't moving.

Cheryl didn't want to kill him, or even hurt him. She just wanted him to go away. She wanted to run her business, please her clients and, maybe someday, get married and have two children. She didn't have time for a boyfriend, giving her all to the business.

"Get out, you perverted son-of-a-bitch." The scissors fell from her right hand to the white, tiled, bathroom floor as Herby pulled a snub-nosed 38 from his shoulder holster and pointed it at her face.

"Get on your knees and suck me, you little tramp." Herby pulled the zipper on his pants down, unbuttoned them and slid them down to his knees, exposing his privates. Cheryl, frozen in shock, couldn't move. Herby grabbed her shoulder with his left hand and forced her weak body onto her jittery knees. "Put it in your mouth and suck it, slowly."

Cheryl's mouth was inches from Herby's penis. She glanced at the scissors on the floor, which had landed about two feet from her right hand. She had to think fast. She grabbed Saunders hardness with her left hand and stroked it with her magic fingers, while leaning forward and grabbing the scissors off the tile floor.

"Put it in your mouth, honey!" Herby had his eyes shut. Cheryl, with scissors clenched tightly in her right hand, jammed them into Saunders' testicles. She yanked them out and pushed them into the side of his penis. Herby screamed. His blood squirted all over Cheryl's naked body. Saunders backed away from Cheryl and grabbed his bloody privates. "You bitch!" The screams became louder. "You ruined me for life, you slut." He looked down at his bloody privates and leaned against the wall, trying to catch his breath. His eyes were wide with fright.

Cheryl got up quickly, rushed to the cell phone in her bedroom and dialed 911. She laid the bloody scissors on her night stand. She grabbed a robe off a chair in her bedroom, put it on and tied it, covering her trembling, naked, bloody body. Herby stood in her bedroom with his gun pointed toward her. The cell phone wasn't working. Cheryl quickly glanced at the face of the cell phone. It read: no service. Herby grinned, "I took care of that cell phone, sweetheart. I have connections everywhere. You would've been better to have sucked me. Now, you will die in your own bedroom." The blood oozed through his tan slacks. His face turned ashen.

Cheryl reached for the scissors. She lunged toward Herby without any recourse and slammed the scissors into his heart. Herby had frozen on her quick approach. He never moved a muscle. Cheryl stabbed him several times, until he lay in a heap on the tan carpet. "Oh, my God! What have I done?" She dropped the scissors and put her hands to her mouth, falling onto her double bed. Sobbing for several minutes, her eyes sprang open. She knew she didn't have a chance in hell of defending herself against the likes of this asshole.

She went quickly to the shower and washed the hurt, sorrow, blood and some of the anguish away. She quickly dried herself, grabbed some clothes from her closet and dresser, and stuffed them in a suitcase her aunt had bought for her at a garage sale. She looked down at Saunders' bloody body to make sure he wasn't moving. His eyes were open wide, along with his mouth.

She threw her makeup in a small bag, placing it in the suitcase. She slammed it shut and put on a pair of jeans, a white, pullover blouse, and a pair of tennis shoes she had bought at Wal-Mart. Her wet hair was a mess, but she ran her fingers through it, picked up her suitcase and headed for the kitchen. She opened the refrigerator and took out three bottles of water, four Clif bars and put them in a plastic grocery bag. She threw four bananas and two pears from the counter into the bag. Grabbing her purse from the kitchen table, she ran out the door. The suitcase went in the back seat and the grocery bag and purse in the front seat. She started her twelve year old, six cylinder Mustang, with 145,000 miles. It ran, but not real well. She had wanted to trade it in this fall.

Chapter 19

FOLLOWING THE ESCAPE

I spent an hour in the creek soaking my aching body. There is something about natural, flowing water easing body pain. Thoughts entered my head as I lay naked in the cool water. Jen and I had come here several times to skinny dip. I looked back toward SAWWS Inc., remembering the first time I had laid eyes on the property. Thousands of hours had been spent trying to save lives all over the world for the last ten years, and now, this. "Why? Why are you punishing me, Lord?" I splashed cool water on my face, washing away the tears that flowed from my eyes. I crawled out of the creek. I hadn't brought a towel so I sat on a log until the warm, night air dried my skin. I smelled better and applied some deodorant. I dressed in the same clothes. I looked at my watch; the dial read: 8:58.

I slept for several hours before being awakened by barking dogs. My heart went to my throat. The dogs, however, seemed to be moving away from me. They were probably chasing a fox. Georgia boys hunt fox at night with hound dogs. My watch read 3:57 a.m. I needed to get to my brother's place.

I had five hundred dollars in cash and carried four credit cards and a debit card. Using my flashlight, I glanced at a picture of Jen. The picture had been snapped when we were at Martha's Vineyard for a long weekend just this past spring. I pressed her picture toward my chest. The tears fell from my eyes. My legs felt weak. I headed toward the Northwest—toward Atlanta. I figured I was going in the right direction. Randy's place is over one-hundred-forty miles away.

6:28 a.m.: The morning sun will crest over the horizon within the hour, giving enough light for me to see several hundred feet in front of me. After walking for several miles down the shoulder of Hwy. 17, an old rattle trap pickup slowed and screeched to a stop alongside of me. The man sitting behind the wheel looked like a hill person from the movie *Deliverance*. "Howdy, sonny." His jaw looked twisted. "Lookin fer a ride are ya?" A large dog rose from the seat and popped his head through the window. His head showed a large mouth, full of very big teeth, and his ears stood straight up. A faint growl filled my ears.

"Hi," I managed to squeak out. I'm bone tired, but sure don't want to get into the cab with the likes of these two. An odor came through the open window, a foul smell, a mixture of body odor and urine; the urine probably came from the dog. It fogged my sinuses. I just stood there, saying nothing, keeping an eye on the dog.

"Ya commin or not? I got to get movin. Headin terd Louisville.

"I'll get in the back." Not waiting for an answer, I climbed in the back. The floor of the truck was covered with straw. Two old, white sows were lying down in the front of the eight foot box. I stayed my distance, standing in the rear all the way to Louisville. The old truck rattled and roared down the highway, never exceeding 45 MPH. The fumes escaping from the rusted-out exhaust reminded me of the hours I had spent in the tunnel.

We entered the city limits of Louisville and I thanked the man. I walked another few blocks and spotted an old Chevy Impala. The sign read:

FOR SALE
1985 CHEV
RUNS GOOD
TIRES INCLUDED
NEED $275.00
WILL TRADE

I walked slowly up to the front porch. A very large dog lay sprawled out on the weathered, front porch. The dog had to weigh over one-hundred-fifty pounds. It could have been related to the one in the old truck. A split second after my left foot touched the first porch step, the dog opened one eye and I froze. "Is anyone home?" I managed to hear myself say. Thirty seconds later the screen porch door opened. A white lady dressed in blue bib overalls, her grey hair twisted into a rat's nest and her bottom front teeth missing, filled the doorway. She weighed twice as much as the dog on the porch. Her breasts were proportioned to the rest of her body: huge. "Whacha wantin'?" Her feet were bare and her toenails were dirty and curled. Large crevasses were on each side of her large, pudgy, oily nose. Her eyes looked like large, brown, glassy stones.

"I was wondering if you'd like to sell your car." I pointed toward the faded, old, blue Impala. With her deodorant and soap definitely not working, the smell forced me to back away from her and the dog.

"Sure do." She looking left and then right. "You wantin' ta trade anything?" Big grin came over her red, blotchy, puffy face. Her remaining teeth were decayed, crooked and stained.

"I will pay you cash." I reached for my wallet.

"I take half cash and the rest you can stick right her." Her large meaty hand went towards her crotch. "I ain't had no lovin in several months now." Her eyes narrowed from the Georgia sun.

"I'll give you $270.00 in cash after I see that she runs."

"She runs real good, mister. The damn coppers have a hard time catchin' me."

I walked toward the car. The windows were down. I spotted two raccoons in the back seat mating. I stopped dead in my tracks. "Yoo-You have a couple of raccoons in the back seat." I squinted from the shiny chrome bumper perched against the wall of the house on the porch, as I looked back at the foul-smelling lady.

"Oh, those damn coons at it again. Just shoo them out when you open the door."

I opened the door and the two coons never missed a lick. I got in, turned the key and the Impala roared to life. I got out and popped the hood. There sat a large engine with a chrome four-barrel carburetor on top. I stepped back and reached under the carburetor with my index finger and pushed on the accelerator; the engine made the car vibrate. I crawled in the car and put the car into drive. The transmission seemed okay. Reverse seemed to work, as well.

I reached for my wallet and took out two hundred dollar bills, one fifty and a twenty and handed it to the fat lady. She grabbed it and stuffed it in between her large, perspiring breasts.

Her hand rubbed her crotch again.

"I need to go." I took off with the two coons in the back seat and the signed title in the glove department. I got out of town and shooed the love birds out of the back seat of the car, figuring they'd be better off away from the previous owner of my new ride.

Chapter 20
ATLANTA

The Impala ran great, as long as you kept it under seventy. Over seventy, it would sputter. I reached Atlanta after lunch. My brother, Randy, lived north of Atlanta, on the Chattahoochee River, on five acres nestled back off the highway. The five acres were set high enough to keep any flood waters from entering his 4000 square foot, all brick home. He had bought this home two years ago in a bankruptcy deal from a financially-strapped bank. The original owner had foreclosed on the property.

I pulled the beat up, old, blue Impala onto his asphalt driveway. I tried to open the door and it stood frozen shut. I pushed with my aching shoulder and nothing. I tried the other door and the same thing occurred. I kicked it with my feet; it sprang open. I crawled out and walked to the front door, leaving the car door hanging open. I rang the door bell and waited for Randy to answer.

My heart ached, wanting to talk, to talk to anyone about the tragic events of the past several days. He never opened the door. I tried the door and it was unlocked. Entering, I shouted, "Randy, Randy, it's Sam." I listened, but there was no sound except for the large wall clock in the foyer clicking off the seconds. Every second became an unknown.

I went through the ranch style house shouting his name. When I came to his den, my heart stopped. Randy sat slumped in his chair with a bullet hole in his forehead. The blood had dried. "For Christ sake, what the hell is going on?" I felt his pulse—no sign of life. He was as dead and cold as ice. My heart swelled. How much more can I take? "Jen, Jen!" I shouted.

I reached for the phone on his desk. I had to call the police. My arm froze before my hand reached the ivory phone. "I can't call the police. His college roommate, Travis Shear, I need to call him. He works for the CIA. I searched through Randy's rolodex. He had two numbers listed, one cell and one home. I dialed the cell number. People say Randy and I sound alike.

The phone rang three times and my heart pounded. "This is Shear."

"Hey Travis, Randy, Randy Abbott." My hands were sweating. I wasn't a good liar.

"R-Randy A-Abbott. H-How are you doing?" His voice cracked on every word.

"Not good! Some asshole tried to kill me yesterday." I felt Randy had been dead for almost a day. I needed to test Travis.

The silence lasted seconds. "H-How? What did he look like?"

"The police have him. His body laid on my garage floor after I blew his ass away."

"The p-police have him. What's his name?" Travis's voice hurried.

"I don't know. I thought maybe you knew something."

"W-why me?"

"I thought you people knew everything. I tried to reach Sam, my brother, but he left for New Zealand yesterday. He called me yesterday from the Atlanta airport before he left. Then, an hour later, this asshole tried to kill me. Why try and kill me? Sam is the one whose life is always in danger."

"Y-you talked to S-Sam Abbott? He, he is ." I now knew the CIA was involved. At least Travis was. Why would Travis want to kill Randy, his best friend?

"I have to go, Travis. I'll call you later."

"W-Wait, Randy. Stay put until I can ." I hung up the phone.

Chapter 21

SOMEWHERE
IN TENNESSEE

took five hundred dollars from Randy's wallet and put it in my
wallet. I stuck his wallet in my pants. Randy and I could pass for
twins, even though I'm ten years older. I grabbed some much-
needed food and jammed it into my mouth. I took a long, hot shower.
Randy was a little smaller than me, but since I'd lost weight, I could
fit into his clothes. I packed a small suitcase, threw a few sundries
in and headed for the blue Impala. I opened the hood and spotted
a disconnected plug wire. I placed the wire on the spark plug, hit
the starter and the big engine roared to life. My gas gauge bounced
on empty.

Stopping at a Shell station, I filled the tank with premium gas.
Disguising my voice, I called the police from a pay phone and let them
know about Randy. I headed for the Impala before the cops could ask
any questions.

Driving north on Interstate 75, I spotted blue lights in my rearview mirror. The State police car gained on me. At least, I figured it was a State Patrol car. I slowed down to seventy; the speed limit posted seventy-five. I'd been doing eighty when I spotted him. "Shit!" The siren screams became louder. The State police car shot by me; my eyes looked straight ahead. My heart left my throat.

I didn't know where to go or what to do, but I needed to get out of Georgia. The Tennessee State line lay some twenty miles ahead. Jen stayed in my mind every mile, along with my employees, and now, Randy.

At ten miles past Knoxville, Tennessee, old blue registered empty. I pulled into another Shell station to fill her up. I checked the oil; it was clean and on full. I grabbed some snacks and a large bottle of water, paid cash, and headed for old blue.

A young, tall, slender girl, wearing sunglasses, leaned against my car. She wore tight, very tight, jeans, and a loose-fitting blouse. Her short-cut, brown hair looked like she had combed it with her index finger. She stood maybe six feet tall. She had a bag hanging on her shoulder. A suitcase and another small grocery bag were lying by her feet. I squinted as I approached her. She never moved, but showed me a soft smile.

"May I help you?" I got a whiff of her cheap perfume as I got within ten feet of her. She sure smelled better than the old lady with the dog.

"I need a ride."

"Where are you going?" I asked.

"Where are you going?" She had a Georgia accent.

I pointed north. "I'm going that way, too," she answered. I saw desperation on her unblemished face.

"Do you have any ID on you?" No way am I taking a minor out of state. She did look older than eighteen, however.

She unzipped her purse and got a driver's license out, handing it to me. I reached for it and saw it was issued from the State of Georgia:

She was twenty-five; her height was 5 feet, 11 inches; and she weighed one-hundred-thirty eight pounds. She lived, or was running away from, Macon, Georgia. Her picture and the person standing in front of me was definitely the same person: Cheryl R. Hanley; hair color, brunette; eyes, hazel.

Handing it back to her, I told her to get in, hoping I wasn't making a mistake, but I needed some company. I hadn't spoken to anyone, except Travis, since that awful day when Jen had disappeared. The other three I tried to forget.

We were only three miles from the Shell station when she spoke. "So, what's your name?"

"My lips froze when I heard her question, but I blurted out, "Sam."

She reached her long arm across the front seat and our hands touched. "My name is Cheryl. I guess you already knew that." Our hands parted. Her hands were soft and they sent a chill through me. "You must work hard for a living. Your hands are really calloused and rough."

I looked at my sore, bruised, calloused, scarred hands and answered, without looking at her, "Yeah, I've worked real hard. W-what do you do?"

"I'm a licensed massage therapist. I've been doing it for four years now."

It remained quiet for several miles. I wanted to tell her everything. The furrows across her young forehead told me she lived under a lot of stress.

I could see from the corner of my eye she wanted to ask me, or tell me, something. Another mile went by before she spoke again. "Sam, you don't really do physical labor for a living. I've been around too many bodies over the last four years. You had an office job, or you were in sales. You don't talk like a laborer." Her eyes stayed focused on me.

"So, how can you be so sure? My hands are laborer's hands." I looked at my hands again.

"Parts of them are hard, while other parts are soft. Your hair is dyed. Your eyes tell me you're running from someone or something." I touched my whiskers with my right hand. "Your nose looks like it may have been recently broken. You're wearing an expensive shirt and driving a beat-up car. Your eyes are red. Have you had a lot of horror come your way?"

Wow! This gal knows me too well. I tried to think of what to tell her. I spotted a scenic view sign and turned my signal on, slowing as I approached the asphalt road. I parked old blue and said, "I need to stretch my legs." I got out of the car and walked around, trying to clear my head. I'm afraid. First, if I tell her what happened, she won't believe me; second, she might tell the police, if she did believe me; third, she is only twenty-five; fourth, she would be the only person who knew except me; and fifth, I might just go to pieces. I pondered for several minutes. My back was to old blue when I heard her voice. "You need to get it off your chest. There isn't anyone here except you and me. Come over here and tell me what's troubling you."

I looked back at her. My legs all of a sudden became weak, and I started moving toward a wooden bench. I sat down hard. My heart was about to unload all the fear, hate, sorrow and unanswered questions that were making my head hurt.

She sat down beside me, placing her hand on my shoulder. The tears ran down my cheeks a second later. "I'm here to listen, Sam. I'm a good listener. I promise it won't go any further than right here."

I unloaded my guts to an unknown, young girl, who probably had enough problems of her own. I told my story in ten minutes, with my crying taking up three minutes. She comforted me during those three minutes of sobbing. I needed the touch, the attention, and the caring. I stood and walked away, taking in deep breaths of Kentucky air. My lungs expanded and my head cleared somewhat during my two minute walk. I turned to walk back to her and she stood right in front of me, her arms extended. I walked right into them. She hugged me and wept.

I found myself holding her tighter. Her loins pressed against mine. "Cheryl, Cheryl, you need to talk to me. I will try and help. We-we can-can maybe help one another."

She nodded and we slowly walked back to the wooden bench. Sitting there, I took her hand in mine and she began: "Sam, Sam I'm a good person. I was brought up as a Southern Baptist. I've wanted to be a massage therapist ever since high school. I think I was just going into my senior year." The tears were flowing from her hazel eyes.

"I worked for a health spa in Macon for two years, 'The Touch of Class'. I made really good money. I worked very hard and my clients loved me. I made enough money to start my own massage business. I called it: 'Magic Fingers Massage'. My business started booming." Her eyes became filled with tears again.

"This past March, a prominent gentleman from Macon, Herby Woody Saunders, came to me and wanted me to give him a massage." She broke down and I held her for several minutes.

She wiped her tears away with her palms and continued, "All my clients, male or female, leave their underwear on, except the women remove their bras. This Saunders guy wanted more than a massage." She made two fists and beat on her thighs. The tears poured from her eyes. Her body became rigid.

"He left quickly and everything seemed okay for several months. It was this past August when I got a letter from the city of Macon. It informed me that my business would have to be shut down in the next thirty days due to too many massage parlors in the city. My place had been pulled from a so-called list of all the parlors in the city." She put her head in her hands, not speaking another word for several minutes.

"I got an attorney and he informed me I would never win the case. If Herby is behind it, which he was, he had more political pull than any man in Macon. The city shut down my business on the exact date they informed me it would be." She stood, arms folded across her breasts.

"My clients wanted me to go to another town. They said they would drive thirty miles if they had to." Cheryl sat with her head tilted down and her hands clasped tightly together.

"I found a cute house to rent down near Fort Valley. I notified all my clients and they promised me they would travel to my new place. Well, everything was going great until one day last week. I get a letter from the County informing me that massage parlors are not allowed in Peach County. I had gotten my permit from the County before I opened. Herby put a stop to it. I was livid." She stood, again, and kicked some stones with her tennis shoes.

The rage in Cheryl's eyes told the rest of the story.

"He came after me. He wanted to have oral sex." She bawled, on the brink of becoming hysterical, without a tear.

A few minutes later, we both got back in the car and drove away, heading to some place unknown. Cheryl rode with her eyes shut and her hands clenched tight. She had left her car with a farmer. She paid him $50.00 to hide the car for at least a week. He promised he'd never tell the damn police a thing. He had had a run in with them several years ago. She hitched a ride to the gas station, where she had leaned against old blue.

Chapter 22
SLEEPING TOGETHER

Stopping in Covington, Kentucky, we fueled old blue and grabbed some much-needed food at a Perkins restaurant. The time: 8:00 p.m. When we walked into the restaurant, two State Patrol officers were sitting in a booth. My body stiffened and Cheryl's eyes widened with fear. One of the officers looked at us with real concern. At least, I thought so. Maybe it was Cheryl they were looking at. She had a great body. We were seated by a middle-aged lady, who gave us our menus and took our drink order. I ordered a Sprite and Cheryl asked for a diet Seven-Up. Our appetites went from starved to not real hungry in two minutes.

We stared at the menus, while keeping an eye on the officers. We didn't get anymore looks from the State Police. I had a tuna sandwich on whole wheat toast and a cup of vegetable soup. Cheryl had a chef salad, with house dressing on the side. I managed to eat all my food, but Cheryl only picked at hers.

Walking out to the car, I asked, "Do you want to get a room and get an early start in the morning?" She shot back a look with "yes" spelled all over it. Though, it took her several seconds before she nodded. I cranked up old blue and headed down the street to a Holiday Inn Express.

We were getting out of the car when Cheryl spoke, in a rather soft voice, "I don't want to sleep alone. Could you get a room with two beds?" I nodded and went inside to the lobby. I registered as Mr. and Mrs. Jerry Stanley; address, Louisville, Ga. The young lady behind the counter gave me a key to Room 248.

I got my backpack and Randy's suitcase from the back seat, while Cheryl reached for her purse and other bags. We took the stairs to the second floor and walked down the hallway to Room 248. I slid the plastic card into the slot and pushed down on the handle. When the door opened, I hit the light switch and a large king bed stared at us. "I-I asked for two queen beds. I-I'll…"

She touched my arm with her long fingers and whispered, "This is okay."

My knees began to buckle. I laid my suitcase on the floor and tossed the backpack on the bed. I turned on the TV. I wanted to know what the news had to say about SAWWS. I hadn't heard a word since that awful day. The people who kidnapped Jen did something to the four radios in the house and the satellite dish. The radio in old blue didn't work. The nine o'clock news was only minutes away from broadcasting.

"Good evening! We have the latest on the SAWWS Inc. investigation. We will go directly to John Andrews in Augusta, Georgia."

"This is John Andrews, coming to you live from the main entrance of the FBI office in Augusta. We have just learned that a body of a woman, who is believed to be Jennifer Abbott, has been pulled from Oconee Lake." My body froze. Jen snapped into my view and my heart rose to my throat, cutting off the air to my lungs. I gasped. "Oconee Lake is located between Atlanta and Augusta. The FBI got a tip from a person who was fishing on the lake and spotted a woman's shoe. The same style shoe was purchased by Mrs. Abbott at Nordstrom's Department Store in Atlanta three weeks ago. It appeared her body had been in the water for over two days. She wore purple Capri pants. DNA samples will be available in two weeks, according to the FBI." I felt light- headed. I thought I'd pass out. Cheryl applied a cold wash cloth to the back of my neck. I sucked in some needed air.

"The FBI has not given us any more information on the employees, who are still missing from SAWWS. Of the forty-three security men that protected SAWWS, thirty have been located and found to have been brutally murdered. The FBI has not given us any information as to who is behind all the murders. The two pilots who were employees of SAWWS were never found." I tried to get off the bed, but my legs wouldn't let me. I wanted to hit something.

"The families of all the employees are banding together and getting petitions signed to send to the President of the United States. They want answers and want to know why the government is so slow in responding to this tragic event. According to some of the families of these missing people, our government has not spoken to them since this massacre occurred, except to ask if they have heard from them. The families of those who were murdered can't believe Sam Abbott has anything to do with the disappearance of his employees." I broke into a sweat. Cheryl reapplied the cold towel to my head and neck.

"The remainder of the employees who worked at SAWWS haven't been located. Some rumors have been floating around. There are tunnels, which were used during the Civil War, in the area of SAWWS Inc. The FBI has yet to dig in the area. The FBI hasn't said whether or not any search was done inside of SAWWS. Everything, according to the FBI, seemed to be in order. The Abbott home sits on five-hundred acres—the same five hundred acres SAWWS Inc sits on. We've been informed everything is intact." My tuna sandwich and soup moved up to my throat.

"The Abbotts, who have been married for ten years, were scheduled to go to New Zealand for twenty one days. They were to leave the day all the employees disappeared." I covered my mouth to keep my supper down. "Sam Abbott, the president and owner of SAWWS, is still missing." My supper wound up in a waste paper basket next to the TV. Cheryl got me a cup of water.

"Sam Abbott's brother, Randy, who lives just North of Atlanta, was found murdered in his home yesterday. There were fresh fingerprints belonging to Sam Abbott in the home. The FBI has issued an all points bulletin for Sam Abbott."

"The Abbotts' bank accounts, along with SAWWS Inc. accounts, were all emptied the day of the disappearance."

"What!" I managed to say in a soft tone.

"The FBI is asking if anyone knows or has seen Sam Abbott to please call them immediately. A five million dollar reward has been offered for any information leading to his arrest. This is John Andrews in Augusta, Georgia."

"We now have the latest on the murder of Herby Woody Saunders, the one time leader of the Democratic Party, from the State of Georgia. Herby Saunders is believed to have been murdered by Cheryl Hanley, a massage therapist. The former clients of Cheryl Hanley have come forward and said that Herby Saunders had stalked Miss Hanley for several months before his death. They also stated her other parlor in Macon had been shut down by Mr. Saunders' political pull, as a result of her refusing to have sex with him. He also attempted to put her out of business in Peach County, Georgia, for the same reason." Cheryl shed some tears—the tears coming from emotion, emotion from hearing her clients believed in her.

I flipped the off button on the remote and the TV went black instantly. I buried my head in my hands and let the hostility enter my body. Memories of the past ten years shot through my head like a cannon.

Chapter 23

NEW ZEALAND—
ELEVEN YEARS EARLIER

D avid Holloway, the financier of SAWWS Inc., sent me to New Zealand to see how they controlled their pollution problem. He had paid for the whole trip and I spent ten days researching and visiting their geo thermo plants. David sensed I needed some time away and knew I wouldn't get another vacation for at least a couple of years.

On day five of my ten-day trip, while sitting in Sid's Deli in Taupo, New Zealand, reading some literature I had acquired from the geo thermo plants, I lifted my eyes from the facts and figures lying in front of me. I rubbed my tired eyes and blinked away the sting. My belly growled a tune of hunger.

The doorway to Sid's Deli came to life. In walked a beautiful lady, with short dark hair, dressed in purple Capris and a white blouse. With her left hand, she reached for her dark sunglasses and lifted them from her face. She stuck an elbow of her dark glasses in between her lustrous, full, red lips. Her eyes met mine and they stayed on me, or at least I thought they were on me. She stopped for maybe thirty seconds; our eyes never blinked. The elbow dropped from her parted, wet lips.

My heart raced and my mouth became dry. I felt a stir in my loins. From what I could see, her body looked almost perfect. I cut a small grin, bringing a sudden smile to her unblemished face. Now my loins began to really ache. The deli only had six tables and all were occupied. They had four outside tables and three of them were full.

When it came to women, I was "Mr. Slow." I knew what I needed to do or say, but my heart and head always ran three minutes behind and the person always got away, or some other dude would step in.

My body rose out of my wooden chair. I stood directly in front of her before my brain told my tongue what to say. "I-I was wondering if you would like to join me?" My heart started pounding like a drum. "My name is Sam Abbott." I stuck my hand toward her belly button. I hadn't dated in several years, or at least I didn't have a steady girl friend, money being my main problem.

She extended her hand and said, with such a tender voice, "Jennifer Snowden, Chicago, Illinois." Her voice sent chills down my spine. The words came out soft, yet energetic.

"I'm from Denver, Colorado." I knew every set of eyes in the deli were on her every move.

"I've skied in Breckenridge. I've been to Denver several times." The twinkle in her eyes stirred up things.

Me, I never skied more than twice in my life and I was known as a butt skier. It seemed easier than using skies. I knew I would lose ground in a hurry. "When was the last time you were in Colorado?" My mouth became dry after the question, hoping it was when she was a little girl. My stomach swelled.

"It has been a few years." I nodded. "I loved the sport, but my right knee didn't feel the same way." I saw a touch of agony in her brown eyes.

My chest loosened up. "I bet you were a great skier." Her legs were long, lean and hung from her shapely posterior. God had taken his time in creating her body. She smiled.

"If you love something, you become good at it." Our eyes locked and the sparks were flying around the deli, like fireworks lighting up Chicago on the Fourth of July. I put my right hand on her shoulder blade to guide her toward the order counter. I felt the warmth radiate up my arm to my head and I knew my face read: code red. She ordered a veggie wrap and a bottle of mango juice. I ordered a ham and Swiss wrap and a bottle of ice tea.

We ate lunch and our eyes stayed locked on each other most of the time. She had a cute smile and I loved her laugh. We spent the rest of the day walking, talking and discussing the goals we thought we wanted. Our day ended up with dinner at Taupo's famous restaurant, "Kiwi Inn". Jennifer had fresh lake trout caught from Taupo Lake and I had a t-bone steak raised in New Zealand. The candlelight dinner, two bottles of dry Chardonnay, and the ambiance created sparks of love. An hour after we finished our meal, we were in my hotel room lying naked, wrapped in each others arms with love juices flowing.

Over the next five days, we fell madly in love with one another. We spent most of our time in bed. Our hearts and bodies couldn't get enough of each other.

Chapter 24
INSEPARABLE

We were inseparable up until the day we left each other at the Los Angeles airport. I headed for Atlanta, Georgia to meet David Holloway. He had found some acreage south of Augusta he wanted me to look at. The acreage would be the new location for our production site.

Jennifer headed for Chicago to go back to work and plan our wedding. We would wait until fall for the wedding, September, in Chicago, after Labor Day, if things could be worked out. We had returned to early spring in the States, having left the end of summer in New Zealand.

Jennifer worked for a large law firm in Chicago. She had been with the firm for five years, working her tail off for a promised partnership in October. She had begun to hate the firm. Her father had warned her when she had taken the job. He had a small law practice in Oakbrook, Illinois, where Jennifer had grown up.

The wedding would be small. A few friends and immediate family would be sent invitations. The reception would be open and would be held at Gargiano's in Oakbrook. Jennifer would check on the availability.

Jennifer, baptized Methodist, and I-I left the Presbyterian Church after graduating high school. I still believed, but my faith had dwindled. We were going to be married in the Snowden's Methodist Church in Oakbrook.

My brother, Randy, would be my best man. I had studied and worked part-time for so many years, my social friends had left the scene. At almost thirty, I had maybe one friend, Robert Hayes, a cop in Denver, the guy who had lent me the money to see Holloway. Robert Hayes and his wife would be attending the wedding. Robert wasn't the smartest oar in the water, but he was the most honest person ever made. Robert had been working homicide for the past four years. He had the body of a Greek God. His name should have been Thor. He stood six feet five and weighed around two-hundred forty pounds. He had played defensive end in high school. Quarterbacks hated to play against him. Everyone called him "Rhino." I called him "Little Rhino."

Chapter 25

AUGUSTA–
ELEVEN YEARS AGO

arrived in Atlanta one hour and twenty minutes late. David had two rooms set up at the downtown Atlanta Marriott. I checked in at 1:00 A.M., Atlanta time. I had two messages: one from Jennifer, telling me how much she missed me already and how much she loved me. My loins ached for her. The expression on my face must have told the night clerk that, because she gave me one of those grins.

The other message came from David. He would meet me at 7:00 A.M. for breakfast. We would leave Atlanta by 8:30 A.M. via his corporate jet. I glanced at my watch; it was 1:15. I hurried to the elevator, wanting to lay my head on a pillow, any pillow.

I managed to crawl out of bed seconds after the phone rang for my wake-up call. I showered, shaved and put on my stain-free, wrinkle-free, tan slacks I had purchased at JC Penney's about three years ago. The cuffs were frayed. The sport shirt I grabbed from my bag was white and had a wine stain on the lower front side, but wouldn't show if I put my Sears, navy, sport jacket on. The navy jacket had a missing button off the right sleeve.

I had informed Jennifer about how poor I was. My parents were of below average income. My father drove a bus for the Denver schools and held odd jobs in between; my mother cleaned houses to help put food on the table. With money earned from washing out the backs of delivery trucks at a local dairy five nights a week after school, I had purchased a $500.00 car, paid the insurance, kept her running and spent money on girls and clothes until going away to college. I managed to save $2000 to attend college and financed the rest with a bunch of loans.

Jennifer's father had put her through Northwestern, where she received her law degree. She had belonged to a sorority and had a new car to drive. Her father, however, had taught her the value of a dollar and how to put it to good use. Jennifer was extremely frugal.

I walked into the dining area and spotted David; his eyes were glued to the Wall Street Journal. "Good morning, David." We were on a first-name basis. David preferred it that way. The time on my trusty Timex read 6:58.

He dropped the paper instantly and stood. Extending his hand, he said, "Good morning, Sam. How was your trip?" His eyes were much brighter than mine. My legs were weak and my eyes burned from lack of sleep from flying for some fifteen hours. I struggled with constipation; in fact, I had been plugged up for two days.

We sat down after a few more words. George, a medium built, black waiter, with a shaven head, took our order. David had dry, whole wheat toast with honey and a large glass of orange juice. I needed to eat, even though I had no idea where the food would go. I ordered two eggs over easy with crisp bacon, whole wheat toast and a large 2% milk to chase it down. I added a plate of fruit with the hope it would break up my blockage.

The conversation was light. We headed for his limo, which had pulled up in front of the hotel less than a minute from the time he had made a call on his cell phone. We arrived at the airport and were aboard his corporate jet right on schedule.

We landed at Augusta airport in less than forty minutes and taxied to another limo waiting on the tarmac.

The fresh air in Augusta made my head feel smaller. Maybe my ears had finally popped. I don't do well in airplanes. The walk to the white limo, less than one-hundred feet at the most, fell quiet. I got in on the right side; David on the left. The doors were opened and shut by two, gigantic, black men dressed in black suits and white shirts. Our driver, also black and bigger than me, appeared tiny compared to the two men we had left on the tarmac. David and I chatted about New Zealand and, of course, the pollution problem we faced in this world.

We arrived at the property, which would become the new company; no name as yet. Jennifer's and my new home would be on the same property. My eyes were skating in every direction. My mouth hung open in awe. David had already walked the property and had toured the two-hundred year old home. He had called me in New Zealand to tell me about the property. When I had told Jennifer, she became ecstatic. We were naked at the time and she began jumping around the room like a young fawn on a sunny, spring day. She had always dreamed of living in a plantation home, with a large garden and flowers everywhere.

We met the realtor, Helen McGuire, at the property. A tall, sophisticated lady, who knew her business, with a Georgia smile and an accent no man could say no to when asked a yes/no question. She was pushing fifty, maybe sixty; colored hair, her face redone, but her hands said differently. Her breasts were not large, however, they made her look like a model in her skin-tight, lavender dress. She listed the property and wanted to sell it to David Holloway, today. Her eyes told us she was winning.

I walked around the tall, Georgia pines and pecan trees like I owned the five-hundred acres. I took long strides and had one hand in my pants pocket. David let me look and dream for half an hour before he said, "Sam, let's look at the house." I told David about Jennifer and our marriage plans. He informed me he had met his wife in May and married her in June of the same year. They still didn't have any children. I never asked why. Jennifer and I are going to fill the house with kids.

The house was humungous compared to the tiny house I had grown up in, in Denver, on Alcott Street. The home needed some attention—windows; paint, inside and out; new appliances; curtains; the hardwood floors needed to be refinished; and, yes, it needed furniture. My God, it'll cost a fortune to furnish the place. I frowned, only because I wanted the best for Jennifer. I hope she understands.

Helen came up behind me, less than five feet from my heels, when she asked me a yes/no question. "Mr. Abbott, do you think Jennifer and you could make this gorgeous house a home to share your love for one another?" Thoughts of Jennifer and me running naked throughout this four thousand square foot home made my loins warm.

The smile on my face as I turned around told Helen McGuire the answer before the word, "yes," rolled out of my dry mouth. She smiled, turned and walked across the large room toward David. Her heals pounded the closing march the closer she got to him.

A handshake sealed the deal. The closing would be next Thursday, a week from today. On the way to the limo, David pointed out where the plant would be. I nodded.

On Thursday, David wrote a check for one point five million and already had an architect lined up, along with a construction company to break ground on the ten thousand square foot plant and office, the Monday following the closing. The man was like Mario Andretti on a race track. He never slowed down and always knew where the next turn would be. His pit crew was the best money could buy and David paid them well, very well. David never used the words: "but, ah, um, maybe, I think, can't, or any four letter words."

My job was to help the architects design the plant and offices. David put me on the payroll at $5000 per month, plus gave me a new Honda Accord. I rented some furniture and found an apartment near downtown Atlanta, only a few minutes from the architect's office. David's only comment, "build it big enough so we can grow." David wanted the plant underground and a security fence no one could enter without going through one main entrance. He saw the curve long before I did.

In four weeks, we had the plans laid out and drawn up for the Jefferson County planning commission to approve. It didn't take me long to figure out David had a tremendous influence on anyone who was around him or dealt with him, personally. He called twice a day requesting updates and giving input. It took them two days, with some persuasion from David's office, to approve them. The ten thousand square foot plant would be two stories high, but secluded under four feet of concrete, rebar, a parking garage and Georgia clay.

Chapter 26
SEPTEMBER WEDDING

O ur wedding day had been set for the last Saturday in September. I saw Jennifer almost every weekend since we had arrived back in the states. She would fly to Atlanta on Friday night and take a red eye back Sunday night. We spent most of our time on top of or between the sheets. Each time she left, it became harder and harder for us to kiss goodbye.

The law firm had put their grips on her. Her production had dwindled. She would tell them about the wedding and our plans one month before. Her father wanted her to tell them immediately; he could feel the pressure they were putting on her.

September came and Robert Hayes and his wife, Sally, and my family, including my brother, Randy, a junior at The Air Force Academy in Colorado Springs, Colorado, were in Oakbrook, Illinois, two days before the wedding. Randy, Robert and I went out and reminisced, while Sally and Jennifer dined together. Randy became the designated driver since he wasn't old enough to drink. Robert and I got plastered on Miller Lite and Dewar's scotch, which Robert had started me on. I still felt the hangover the morning of the wedding, a day and a half later. I did remember to pay back Robert the money he had loaned me.

The First Methodist Church filled with many relatives and friends of Jennifer's and the Snowden's. I had less than a handful attend. David and his wife couldn't be there as they were at a meeting in Tokyo.

Jennifer's maid of honor, Sue Lewis, her friend since grade school, wore a lemon chiffon dress. All eyes were entrenched on her. Her smile would make any man soften. When she spoke, her voice radiated the room. Also a lawyer, she worked for a small firm in Chicago.

Jennifer looked gorgeous in her white wedding gown. Her shoulder length, dark hair, dark brown eyes and her full red lips made my heart jump, as she walked down the aisle with her father. All eyes were glued on Jennifer, while she so gracefully strode toward the front of the church.

The minister's white robe covered three quarters of his plain, navy, three button suit.

Randy and I wore rented, black tuxedos, with white, silk shirts. A stream of perspiration ran down the middle of my back when Jennifer's father gave her hand to me. My palms were wet, my mouth dry, as we stood in front of the Reverend Carl Stokes, a middle-aged man with a dynamic voice.

The short ceremony consisted of one song, sung by another friend of Jennifer's, Kathy Wilcox, who sang "The First Time." Thoughts of Jennifer and me in Taupo, New Zealand, flowed through my head like wind covering a wheat field.

The service ended and the minister gave those final words, "You May Kiss the Bride." We kissed passionately, like we always did. The sparks bounced around the church.

We held the reception at St Andrew's Country Club, where a live band, open bar and sit down dinner awaited our arrival. All the guests and relatives had arrived, except Randy, Sue, Jennifer, Jennifer's mother and father and my mother and father and me. Pictures always take too long.

Entering the ballroom, Robert handed me a Dewar's on the rocks, accompanied with a slap on the back and a big hug. He kissed Jennifer on the cheek and said, "Jennifer, if ever you need anything other than money, call me." His grin covered the whole front of his face. "Sam, here, …" His large paw gripped my shoulder. "Sam, here, is the greatest, but if he ever steps out of line, you call me."

"I will do that Robert, but I rather doubt he will get out of line." Her brown eyes made my whole body melt as she looked into my eyes. I put my arm around her waist, pulled her toward me and kissed her on the cheek.

"Jennifer and I want to have several children, grandchildren and great grandchildren. We want nothing but Abbotts running around the house."

"Don't forget Rocky," Jennifer chimed in.

"Rocky?" I looked at Jennifer. "Rocky is Jennifer's heart and soul," I said with a grin.

"He has had all my heart and soul. Now he has to share with you, Sam." Her eyes were wet.

We danced the night away and by two a.m. we had loaded a ton of gifts from the ballroom into my parent's rental car, a Ford Fusion, and Jennifer's parent's new Lexus.

Jennifer and I headed for the Marriott downtown Chicago, where we had a suite for the evening. We were catching a ten a.m. flight to the Caymans for a week's stay.

Chapter 27
FIRST CHRISTMAS

David and his wife, Joan, had given us a $30,000 gift certificate to the finest furniture store in Georgia. Jennifer picked out everything and wrote out all the thank you notes by the second week after returning from the Caymans. She hired two painting contractors to paint the inside and outside of the house. All I said was "wow." She was like David—she saw the turn long before it became visible.

She had the four bathrooms re-plumbed and new fixtures and cabinets installed. New cherry cabinets and appliances were put in the kitchen. Jennifer organized everything, while I worked twelve hours a day, six days a week, getting things lined up for the new manufacturing plant and organizing and hiring a staff. David stressed the hiring of top-notch security people would be far more important than top-notch people for the manufacturing. Great security people don't have to be trained, but manufacturing people do. I never realized our product would require that much security. I never saw around the curve.

Christmas came and my parents and Jennifer's parents, along with my brother, came to our place for the holiday season. Jennifer had the house all decorated. All the molding had been refinished. I found it simply amazing. I took off one day, Christmas. The rest of the time I spent planning, structuring and organizing my staff. Christmas Eve day, 4:40 in the afternoon, is when I interviewed and hired Virginia, my secretary.

Jennifer and I tried to start a family for two years and finally decided one of us had a problem. We went to a specialist in Atlanta and ran tests. Jennifer was not capable of having any children. It took her several years to get over it. I suggested we adopt. She wouldn't hear of it—that being the only time in our marriage we had disagreed on anything major. She still had Rocky and she had her orchids. Her orchids became her family.

David and I had an agreement drawn up by his lawyers. He financed the whole project, including the five hundred acres, the house, manufacturing facility, security fence, and payrolled all employees for two years. He also continued to pay me $5000 per month. The total was in excess of $32,000,000. After two years, I would get fifty percent of the profits and had to manage and pay all expenses. After five years, he would no longer be a partner.

David turned a $32,000,000 investment into a $60,000,000 profit in five years. He never slowed down, nor questioned my judgment, only offered advice, usually on a weekly basis.

I paid cash for the 5000 foot landing strip, the hangar and the corporate jet, eight years after SAWWS Inc. became operational. The cost of the jet, landing strip and hangar totaled over $28,000,000.

Ten years after the first vile of serum sold, SAWWS Inc. had a cash flow of over $485,000,000. SAWWS Inc.'s net worth was in excess of $800,000,000. Jennifer and I owned SAWWS Inc. lock, stock and barrel.

Jennifer and I never took a vacation during those ten years. We did take several long weekends to various places after SAWWS Inc. had acquired the jet.

Chapter 28

OCTOBER – WAKING UP

woke up staring at the ceiling; panic set in instantly. The nightmares were bouncing around inside my head. Cheryl had her right arm across my chest; her right leg entwined with my right leg. She breathed slowly. We were both dressed in our same clothes, which were now wrinkled. I looked at my watch and the time read 5:28. I glanced toward the curtains and the sun wasn't up yet. The clock on the night stand read the same time as my watch. My empty stomach growled. My mouth tasted like spoiled tuna.

I gently took Cheryl's arm and removed it from my chest. She rolled the opposite direction, gave a soft moan and never woke up. I swung my legs slowly and my feet hit the floor. I stood up; my legs were still asleep. I went to the bathroom and threw cold water on my face. The image in the mirror showed a disgusting human being.

After looking in the mirror for several minutes, I rummaged through my backpack for some clean clothes. I headed for the shower and ran hot water on my neck and back trying to uncork the aches I still had from shoveling Georgia clay.

My eyes were sunk into my head. My nose bent to the left. I still had swelling and purple skin under my left eye and on the side of my nose. No one would ever recognize me, no way.

I opened the bathroom door, slowly. Cheryl stood by the bed, her back to me. "Good morning, Cheryl," I said quietly. Her hair was twisted from the pillow and the restless night she had had. We were alive, but stood in fear.

She turned slowly, gave me a quick smile and said, "Good morning, Sam."

"I'm hungry. I need to get some food in me." Cheryl hadn't moved yet.

"Okay, I need to shower." She reached up and ran her long fingers through her hair, shook her head and walked leisurely to the bathroom.

We checked out. After screening the streets for cops, I drove to a McDonald's two blocks away. We went inside and stood in a line ten people deep. We never spoke a word until a Hispanic girl, who looked to be maybe sixteen, asked for our order.

We ate quickly. Every time our eyes met they told the other person how uncertain we were about where we were going and who we could trust. Certainly, the FBI and the CIA could hardly wait till I contacted Robert or David or Jennifer's parents. I didn't want to put them in harm's way. My father had passed away two years ago and my mother resided in a nursing home in Arvada, Colorado. She had Alzheimer's. I'm glad in a way my dad's not here and my mom would never be aware of what had happened.

Old Blue ran great while heading West on Interstate 74. We spotted a few State Patrol cars heading in the opposite direction. We were in and out of Indiana before noon, entering the Corn Belt State of Illinois shortly after two.

The miles went by fast. I spotted Intrastate 57 and headed north toward Chicago. We arrived in downtown Chicago at 7:00 p.m. I didn't know what or why I went to Chicago, but I felt we could hide out better in a larger city.

We checked into another Holiday Inn, with Old Blue left in a parking garage under the hotel. We checked in as Paul and Nancy Spencer from Godfrey, Georgia. I wanted the Georgia license plate to correlate with our address. Our room on the tenth floor overlooked Lake Michigan and had two queen beds. We ordered room service.

Cheryl hadn't said fifty words all day. She looked out the window at the blue water of Lake Michigan. "Sam, I'm scared." She turned toward me, her arms folded across her breasts. "What are we going to do? We will have every cop in the United States looking for us." I thought I spotted a tear trickle down her cheek.

"Cheryl, I wish I had an answer. I need to think about it for a few days." I walked toward her. She walked toward me and we embraced. I could feel her heart beating against my chest. She trembled and held me tighter. All we had was each other. We couldn't use a credit card, couldn't write a check, couldn't call anyone we knew, and we were running from the FBI and the CIA, not to mention every cop in the United States. We only had a little over six hundred dollars cash between us. Time was running out. Nobody pays cash for a room. I had to use one of my credit cards for security until we checked out, hoping no one looked at the name. Then, I would pay cash the same way I did in Covington, Kentucky.

The food came and we both ate in silence. At 9:00 p.m., we turned the TV on to catch the news on WGN. "We have the latest on SAWWS Inc. and the disappearance of over one-hundred-sixty employees. The FBI has found the bodies of one-hundred-twenty-three men and women buried in a tunnel approximately two hundred feet from the plant. They were buried alive, according to the County Coroner's Office. Sam Abbott, however, was not found in the mass burial. The FBI believes Mr. Abbott led his employees into the dark tunnel, had poisonous gas explosives set, and used a remote to set them off. An all-world bulletin has been issued, with a twenty-five million dollar reward offered for any information on the whereabouts of Sam Abbott."

"I bet they're using my money to put up the reward money for me," I said, shaking my head.

"It hasn't been determined yet whether Jennifer Abbott's body is the body pulled from Oconee Lake two days ago. They were unable to check dental records because all the victim's teeth were missing." My supper rose in my throat. "The victim's body was the same size as Jennifer Abbott's. All jewelry worn by the victim either had been taken or the victim didn't wear any." My heart stood still. "The Abbotts were supposed to depart on a flight to New Zealand the day Sam Abbott's brother, Randy, was shot in the head."

"Bastards!" I picked up a pillow from the bed and fired it across the room, striking a floor lamp, smashing the globe and light bulb. Cheryl reached for my arm as I tried to punch my fist into the wall.

"Sam, Sam, you can't," Cheryl screamed. I pulled back when the TV announcer said: "David Holloway, the computer genius and the second wealthiest man in the world, who had financed the startup of SAWWS Inc., has made this statement:

'Ladies and gentleman, I want to convey to you Sam Abbott had nothing to do with the disappearance of his wife and the employees of SAWWS Inc. I'm putting together the best investigators money can buy to find out who is behind this mass murder. Sam Abbott's life has been in danger for more than nine years. The families of the victims need and want to know how this could have happened.'

"We understand Mr. Holloway will be paying for all burial expenses and will make sure the families of the victims are taken care of." I threw up my supper.

"Continuing, we have additional information on the Herby Woody Saunders case. Mr. Saunders', the one time Democratic Chairman for the state of Georgia, murderer, Cheryl Hanley, was spotted in Texas. The FBI has gotten a lead that a person fitting her description was seen in Waco, Texas. The reward for Cheryl Hanley has risen to $1,000,000."

"Sam, what if we go to Canada?" Her eyes were wet and her pupils swelled with fear.

"Cheryl, Canada would extradite us in a heartbeat. We need to get new identifications. You need to, maybe change the color of your hair and the style." I looked at her and said nothing else.

Several minutes later she looked in the mirror, ran her fingers through her hair and said, "What do you think about auburn and I'll cut it real short?" She turned around and pulled her hair back with her hands, showing me how it would look short.

"Okay, yeah, auburn will be fine." I stood up and moved slowly toward the window. "I'm going to try and find someone to give us new identifications. We need credit cards, driver's licenses, and new social security numbers."

"Where are you going to get this done and how are you going to get it done?" I turned and saw her lips munched together. The furrows on her forehead grew deeper.

"I'll find someone on the street. They know where and how to get these things done." I was guessing. I had seen it in the movies several times and figured it must be true.

Chapter 29
CHICAGO

The next morning, after showering and dressing, I wanted to venture out on the streets of Chicago to seek out someone, anyone, who could give me some information on how to get new identifications. Cheryl was awake and said, "I want to go with you."

"I really don't think you should. You should get your hair cut and change the color." I tried to smile, but my heart wouldn't allow it.

"Alright, but how long will you be gone?" She showed me her pouted lips.

I shook my head, glanced at my titanium watch and looked out the large window. "I'll be back by lunchtime." Maybe I could hock my watch.

The cool breeze off the lake opened my sinuses and my nose began to drip. Every step I took, I saw Jennifer. She was dressed in her lilac robe. My pace picked up. I had to get her out of my mind. Thoughts of her were driving me insane. I spotted a Catholic Church a hundred yards away. "A priest, yes, a priest," I said out loud. "You can trust a priest. Can't you?" I looked up into the heavens. My pace picked up. The time was 8:30 a.m.

I entered St. Michael's Catholic Church. The sanctuary sat empty, except for three nuns kneeling in front of the Virgin Mary. I walked toward the front of the sanctuary and took a seat four rows from the front on the left.

A chill ran down my back when I felt a hand on my shoulder. Afraid to turn around, my heart pounded. Three seconds went by and a deep voice said, "Excuse me, sir, but this is where I pray everyday at this time."

My heart started up again. I only nodded, not showing him my face. I stood up and moved down the pew. My legs were weak from fright. I sat down, again, and waited. I tried to think of how to tell the priest my problem so he would believe me.

One of the nuns, who had been praying earlier, came up the aisle to my left. I slid quickly towards her. "Excuse me, but I wish to speak to a priest, in private."

"Okay, confession is this way." She pointed toward the rear of the sanctuary.

"No, no confession." I shook my head. "I just want to talk to a priest."

She looked into my pleading eyes. "Follow me, sir." She led me into this room covered with oak, except for the off-white painted upper walls and ceiling. The nun motioned for me to have a seat on the right side of the table. The room was small, cold, still, and windowless. There were four chairs and a table that matched the floor and the walls. I waited for what seemed like an hour, checking my watch every few minutes. Had they called the police?

Forty-eight minutes had passed since I had entered this oak room when the large, solid oak door slowly swung open. A man in priestly garb filled the doorway. But, I got this feeling in my gut he wasn't a priest. The face, the face was not a priest's face. His face appeared rugged, gnarled, and his eyes looked hard. He was big enough to play offensive tackle for the Minnesota Vikings, with large shoulders and a thick neck. His large hands hung below his robe. His fingernails were clean; hands were unscarred. Well, maybe a priest, or maybe a cop. Adrenaline ripped through my veins.

"Sister Irene said you wanted to talk to a priest. I'm Father O' Malley." His voice sounded soft, not hard like his face and body.

I put my sweaty hands on the table and pushed myself up into a standing position. I stood three inches shorter than him. I wanted to bolt for the door, but the table and the priest were in my path. I had neither the strength nor the will to try. I didn't know where to start or whether I should say anything. My mouth felt dry, like two-week old toast. I looked at the priest and he stared back. His large forearm extended from his robe and gripped my calloused hand. His hand covered mine completely. "Ah-Ah I need someone I can trr-trust." I wanted those words back in my mouth.

A quick smile lit up his rugged face. "Please, have a seat. What you say to me will never leave this room." He pulled out a chair and sat his huge body down, laying his enormous arms on the table. The swelling in my chest subsided. I sat down hard in my chair, which made a screeching sound when the chair slid on the oak floor. I hoped I hadn't scratched the floor.

I looked at his blue eyes, which had softened somewhat and decided I needed to unload.

I told Father O' Malley everything. He never spoke, except to say, "I've read about SAWWS Inc. in the paper."

After I drained my head and heart of all the stored up hate, frustration, and misfortune, I slumped back in my chair and stared at my hands lying on the table. "Father, I need a drink of water." My words came out a little stronger than a whisper.

His right hand went under the table; my eyes were glued to that arm. What—A gun? A tape recorder? His hand came back up momentarily before he spoke. "Mr. Abbott, you have come to me today to tell me about your anguish, loss and concern for your life. Mr. Holloway has shown his belief in you." He paused several seconds. "I believe what you have told me here this morning. I have some friends you can trust who will help you."

"Father, I-I need different identification and credit cards so I can survive until I can get my name cleared. I have less than $500.00. The people" I wasn't sure. "Only God knows who took all my money."

"My friends will help you." The door opened and Sister Irene stood there. "Sister, please bring a pitcher of water, two glasses, paper and a pen." My heart rate slowed down when I realized he had pushed a button under the table.

"Yes, Father." She quietly shut the door behind her.

"Are you Catholic, Mr. Abbott?"

I shook my head and said, "No, Father O'Malley." My eyes dropped.

"I take it you're a Christian then?" His blue eyes squinted.

"Ah, yes, Father. I was baptized in a Presbyterian Church."

Sister Irene knocked on the large door and Father O'Malley took a silver tray with two glasses and a pitcher of water with his right hand and set it on the table. In his left hand, he had a note pad and pen. He poured a full glass of water and handed it to me. He then poured another glass and sat down with pad and pen in front of him.

"Mr. Abbott, what kind of car are you driving?"

"I have an old blue Impala. I bought it off a lady in Georgia. It runs great." I had just drunk a half glass of water.

"Is the car at the hotel? If so, I'll have someone tow it away. I will see to it that you get another car."

"Yes, but I only have $500.00 dollars." He never looked at me.

"You are traveling alone, I take it?" His big, pale, blue eyes peered above his reading glasses.

"Ah. No sir. I mean Father." His eyes squinted. He laid his pen down and folded his arms across his large chest.

"Do you wish to tell me about your traveling companion, or is there more than one?" His eyes were glued to mine.

I told him the whole story about Cheryl. His arms remained folded the entire time. His eyes never left mine. I'm not sure they ever even blinked. After I had finished, he unfolded his arms and laid them on the table. He then put his hands together in front of his head, with elbows on the table, and bent his head. I believed he was praying for me and Cheryl, or maybe for himself. I wasn't sure, but my stomach met my throat and I reached for the half-full glass of water, gulping the rest of it down.

"Mr. Abbott, you are in great danger and, now, you have a companion who is wanted for murder, even though you believe she had to kill someone in order to survive." He rubbed his large hands together. "I understand your concern for the young lady, but this presents an even greater danger for you."

I nodded, but never spoke.

He rose from his chair. "I'll be back in a few minutes. I need to make a few phone calls." He stared at me for what seemed like a minute, then continued, "Mr. Abbott, why don't you go into the sanctuary and kneel down and pray. I will meet you back here in thirty minutes." He checked his watch and I looked at mine.

"Yes, Father. Father, you must trust us. We have no one we can turn to." I knew I was begging, but I felt better saying it.

Chapter 30
NEW IDENTITIES

Before leaving, I looked up at Father O'Malley and said, "Father O'Malley, I need a big favor." His eyes narrowed. "Father, would you please try and contact Mr. Holloway and let him know I am okay."

Father O'Malley stared at me with narrowed eyes. "I'm not sure it's a good idea. You'll be putting him in danger. He's trying to get your name cleared. I think it best we leave it alone for right now."

I nodded, but didn't like the answer he had given me. We parted company at 11:15 a.m. I had a manila envelope in my right hand, which contained our instructions. Father O'Malley briefed me and hugged me goodbye. "May God be with you today, tomorrow and always."

"Thank you for everything you have done. I shall never forget what you have done for me and Cheryl." My eyes were wet. I would have written a check right then and there for a million dollars to his Parish, but I decided to wait until another time. Besides, I didn't have any money in the bank.

I almost ran to the hotel to give Cheryl the good news.

At six blocks from the Hotel, I heard "Sam! Sam!" My blood stopped flowing in my veins for a few seconds. The voice came from behind me—a male voice. I kept the same pace, afraid to stop or turn around. I didn't recognize the voice, or I didn't think I did. No, it wasn't Father O'Malley. "Sam, it's me, Travis." I heard his steps behind me. My heart stopped, but my feet were still moving. How could he recognize me? My fists became clenched. It didn't sound like Travis, or at least I didn't think so, but then nothing had been clear since that awful day.

Jennifer's face appeared in front of me. "Jen, Jen" I managed to whisper from my dry lips. The steps behind me grew louder and louder.

"Sam, wait. I have some great news." That voice did not belong to Travis Shears. I continued my pace. The man, now beside me, said, "I'm sorry." He stared at me a moment. "I thought you wer-were someone else."

I never said a word, just tried to get my heart beating again. My lungs hurt from lack of oxygen. I wondered how much longer I'd have to run, have to hide, have to be somebody else, have to be broke. "Oh, God, please help me."

Cheryl was sitting in the room when I arrived. I closed the door behind me and locked it. Walking toward the bed, I opened the manila envelope. My hands were still trembling from the encounter with the man on the street. "Sam, you're shaking." She put a hand on each of my shoulders. "What is that?" Cheryl asked.

Her touch helped control my shaking. I looked up at her. "Your hair, I like it." She gave me a quick smile, as she ran her fingers through her reddish, short hair. Her hair looked to be no longer than maybe one and a half inches.

"I saw a priest, a Father O'Malley, and he will help us. These are our instructions." I pulled them from the envelope and several pieces of paper fell on the carpeted floor by my feet. I reached down and grabbed them. Cheryl sat next to me on the bed.

The first page informed us to stay in our room until someone came to take our pictures and get our measurements. This person would be a lady named Rene. She would have black hair and wear a red jacket with silver buttons. Our Illinois driver's licenses would be ready the following morning. This same lady would bring them, along with a credit card with a $3000.00 limit and an expiration date in six months. Our names would be changed to Trevor L. Moss and Josephine R. Rogers. "Josephine was my aunt's name," Cheryl blurted out.

We would have a Motorola cell phone, a phone charger and Verizon would be our carrier. The phone would be registered under another name not revealed. Rene would bring the phone with the licenses.

A 2004, blue, Honda Accord would be in the hotel parking garage. Again, Rene would bring the keys to our room. The Honda would be registered under an ABC Car Rental company. All papers would be in the glove department.

A folded map gave us directions to Payson, Arizona. I looked at Cheryl; her eyes met mine. I saw a slight twinkle. "I've never been to Arizona," I said. Looking at the map, my index finger traced the yellow magic marker line from Chicago to Payson.

"I've never been outside of Georgia until a few days ago." Her face showed strain. "One day I went to Alabama with my momma to see my Aunt Bessie in Pottersville," Cheryl said, before she ran her finger across the map to an unknown area.

"Cheryl, you call me Trevor and I will call you Jo." Our eyes met and stayed glued to each other for several seconds.

She smiled, threw her arms around me and whispered in my right ear, "Okay, Trevor." I held her close until the warmth of her body made my face flush.

I read the rest of the information and found out we were staying in Rolla, Missouri the first night and Albuquerque, New Mexico the second night, reaching Payson on the third day. We would be staying in private homes and all meals would be furnished. A sheet from Map Quest, included in the packet, showed each home's address. No names were mentioned. They were to be notified about our arrival. A thought hit me: Pictures of us would be sent to these people.

The paperwork instructed me to get my hair cut and beard trimmed prior to picture taking. The barber, a short man with a blue coat, would be at our room at 4:00 p.m. today. I reached up and ran my fingers through my shabby beard. Jo looked at me and held my hairy face with her long, muscular fingers. "You could use a trim. I'm not sure about the burr cut, though." Her fingers slowly ran its course, massaging my scalp, while her hot breath covered my face.

"You have great hands, Jo." I slumped into a half trance, while her fingers tried to take away the hurt that had engulfed my head. Before I knew it, my forehead was lying on her breasts and my body went limp.

I managed to raise my head and read the rest of the information. Jo's fingers continued to massage the back of my neck. I read on. When we reach Payson, we are to call a telephone number listed and someone will meet us to give us our itinerary. The cell phone should only be used in an emergency and to contact the man in Payson. We were given three emergency telephone numbers to be used while on our trip, only in the designated States.

All of our old identifications, along with anything else traceable, were to be given to the lady with the red jacket with silver buttons. That included my gun. I probably would never use it, but the thought of not having it scared the crap out of me. All of our clothes, personal items, identifications, jewelry, including my watch, wedding ring and anything else the black-haired lady thought needed to be confiscated, would be taken and put somewhere safe. At least, I hoped so. My wallet and Jennifer's picture would be—"Oh!" My left hand went to my mouth, "My God."

Chapter 31

MY HEART FROZE

Someone knocked on our door. I'd been rereading all the information for the tenth time. I had to memorize every detail as all the information would be taken from us by the lady with the red jacket. My heart froze. I looked at my watch and it was 3:59 p.m. I forced myself to a standing position. Jo sat looking out the window and upon hearing the knock, spun around. Her eyes read *frightened.* I walked toward the door. The sweat oozed from the pores on my palms.

I looked through the peephole. A short man in a blue coat stood looking up at the peephole waiting for me to open the door. I opened the heavy, fireproof door. He looked at me and said in a husky voice, "Your name Trevor Moss?"

I nodded, stepped back and let him in, shutting the door behind him. He carried a small, black bag. He checked around the room and then went into the bathroom. His cheek twitched before he said, "We'll do it in here." He laid the bag on the vanity and unzipped it, pulling out two pairs of scissors, hair clippers, a black comb, a small hair brush, a small vacuum and a small brush to clean the clippers.

After twenty minutes, he had trimmed my beard, given me a burr cut, cleaned his clippers with the small brush, vacuumed up all my hair, packed his things neatly back into his black bag and gone out the door. The only words he spoke were after I had opened the door and let him in: "We'll do it in here." I never said anything to him.

I studied myself in the mirror and, without a doubt, I looked better, maybe even younger. Jo joined me in the bathroom. "Trevor, you look so much better. I hardly recognize you."

I smiled as she ran her hand across my thick stubble. She kissed me lightly, high on my cheek, with her left hand pressed against my other cheek. Her breasts were pushed against my arm. My loins ached. My head wanted her. My heart stopped me cold. The view of Jennifer iced my thoughts, instantly. Jo knew immediately, but said nothing, just stroked the back of my neck with her long fingers.

A loud pounding at the door erased any thoughts we might have had. "It's the police. Open up at once." The pounding terrified both of us. I tried to move, but my body froze. Jo's face turned white. Her eyes widened, never blinking. The loud voice came again. "Open up at once. This is the police." More pounding came, only this time much louder.

I dragged myself toward the door, knowing our fate could be seconds away. The damn credit card I used for security at the front desk. How could they find us so quickly? There's no way they could know— unless the priest—no way. My hand reached the French door handle and unlatched the safety chain. I looked at Jo, who was stowing the papers and the manila envelope under the bed covers. I nodded and pushed down on the handle. I pulled open the door. Greeting me were three men, their guns drawn. Two of the men were dressed in uniform; the other in a navy sport coat, tan slacks, blue shirt and tie. All three were taller and bigger than me.

"Get your hands up and lean against the wall. You, too, miss." Jo froze. "Move it, lady. Now!" She hadn't moved. A uniformed cop grabbed her arm and shoved her against the wall. "Get your hands up." Her arms were shaking. The cop placed her hands above her head and against the wall. He kicked her feet apart. "Don't touch her, officer. We need to get a female officer up here," the plain clothes cop said.

I stood with my feet three feet apart, my hands flat against the wall. Two hands ran from my burr cut to the bottom of my feet. "He's clean," a uniformed cop reported.

The plain clothes cop's cell phone rang. He reached in the side pocket of his sport coat and pulled out the phone, flipping the cover and said, "Hanson here." Thirty seconds later, he said, "You're sure you have the right people?" He flipped his cover shut and dropped the cell phone in his coat pocket. "I'm sorry, folks. We got a bad lead. They just caught the people we were looking for. We apologize, but we have to check out every lead. The people we were trying to apprehend are killers. We have to do our job. Again, we are sorry. You folks have a nice day." When the door shut behind us, Jo and I collapsed on the bed.

We held each other. Both of us trembled. Jo spoke first. "Trevor!"

"Yes."

"I don't know if I can do this. When will it end?" I could feel the heat from her body. "That scared the be-jesuses out of me. Hold me, Trevor."

"I know. Hopefully, we'll get everything resolved."

We embraced on the bed, our bodies pressed against one another. Her trembling lasted for several minutes. Our mouths met and we kissed. Her lips were dry. Was I trying to console her or did I really want to make love to her? We kissed again and her lips became moist. Her tongue touched mine. Our bodies pressed tighter.

The phone rang and we both jumped. On the fourth ring, I managed to pick the receiver up. "Hello."

A female voice on the other end wanted to know if we needed anything from the bar. They were having a special today. "We have two for one, with several choices of hors-d'oeuvres." I put my hand over the mouthpiece and asked, "Jo, do you want anything from the bar? They have hors-d'oeuvres, also."

"Okay, I'll have a glass of red wine and whatever they have." She sat up on the bed with her long legs crossed in front of her, Indian style.

I smiled. "Yes, we will have some red wine and a Dewar's on the rocks, with a splash of water." I put the cordless phone down on the night stand next to the bed. Jo threw her arms around my neck.

"Maybe if we get drunk enough, we can block out our nightmares," Jo said. Her body remained rigid.

"I have to admit, a scotch right now would surely ease my tension."

"I'll give you a massage later. I promise you'll feel much better." She grinned, but lost it immediately.

The five o'clock news was on the TV. "We have some vital information on the SAWWS Inc. murders. Jennifer Abbott, the wife of Sam Abbott, has been identified as the victim pulled from Lake Oconee just last week. DNA results are conclusive. The FBI in Atlanta informed us today." My heart sank to the floor. My body ran ice cold in seconds. I wanted to throw up, but had nothing in my stomach. Jo had her hands on my temples immediately.

"Mr. Snowden, Jennifer Abbott's father, had these words to say after finding out his daughter was the victim." I raised my head to watch Jen's father speak.

"Jennifer's mother and I want to let everyone know we don't believe for a second that Sam Abbott had anything to do with our daughter's death or the death of any of his employees. I feel he has been captured." His voice cracked with every word. A pause in his voice silenced the room. "God only knows who, why, or how these brutal crimes were done. Sam is the brains behind SAWWS. He has either been murdered or he is on the run because our government has yet to come up with any evidence in this horrific crime. Sam, if you by any chance are listening to this news cast, please watch your backside. I'm working everyday with David Holloway on this tragic ordeal. I'm here to tell you, we will get to the bottom of this."

Jo's finger tips were pushing and stroking my temples. If it weren't for her, I'd probably shoot myself. I can't lose anymore. My wife, my brother and all my employees murdered. I've saved thousands of lives over the last ten years and, now, they destroy everything. Who are they? I jumped up from the bed and went in the bathroom, locked the door and coughed up slimy bile. I cried for several minutes. I was sitting on the floor of the bathroom with my head in my hands when Jo's voice came through the door. "Trevor, Trevor what can I do?" I said nothing. "Trevor, you can't do it alone. Let me help. We have no one except each other. I need you, Trevor. Please answer me. Oh, God, please help me."

I crawled to the door and unlocked it. Jo pushed it open slowly and then embraced me. "Trevor, I was afraid you—oh, God, hold me."

I got myself up off the floor and threw cold water on my face. Looking in the mirror, I saw a startled man.

A loud knock at the door rattled me. "Go away, damn it. Leave us alone."

"Trevor, it's probably room service." She rushed toward the door. It was room service. I just stared at the young man who had brought our wine, scotch and hors-d'oeuvres. He looked at me and his eyes widened as he sat the tray down on the large dresser.

My image in the mirror above the dresser looked pathetic. I had bile splattered on the front of my burgundy sweater and my eyes were blood shot. I took off the sweater and threw it across the room.

"Here, Trevor, have some scotch. You'll feel better," Jo said, as she put the glass of scotch in my hand and moved my hand toward my lips, as if I were a baby.

I took a swig and almost choked. Jo beat me on my back. I wanted to die, but something in my heart was telling me to fight. I wish I could see the curves. Right now, I can't see the straightaway. David, I need your help.

Chapter 32
LOSING
SELF CONTROL

W e sipped our drinks and munched on the hors-d'oeuvres. The silver tray held three different kinds of hors-d'oeuvres: Egg rolls filled with spinach; chicken wings with a mustard sauce; and several raw vegetables with a French onion dip. After the second scotch and spending an hour rehearsing, I hoped my brain remained capable of handling the storage of information. I used to be really good at comprehension, but lately I didn't trust myself.

Jo read everything as soon as I finished. She laid the papers down and walked over to me. I was standing in front of the window, staring into space, picturing my employees, Jennifer, my brother, and my parents as I remembered them. Her arms slid through my limp arms and she cupped my breasts. She laid her head on my left shoulder and pulled me tightly against her. I felt the warmth of her body, the softness of her breasts against my back. I needed her love. I had no one else left.

My groin ached. She kissed my ear and her hands fell toward the forked part below my waist. "Trevor, I need your love." We didn't know how much longer our freedom would last before the cops found us.

I took her long, slender, strong hands and laid them on my hardness. Our hearts began to pound. I turned around and she melted into my open arms, pushing against my groin. Our wet lips parted and our mouths opened to each other. The temperature in our bodies rose quickly as I led her toward the king size bed.

Flashes of Jennifer bounced in my head as I fondled Jo's breasts. She had her hands on me, stroking gently. What little self control I had left vanished immediately. She loosened my belt buckle. I had her blouse unbuttoned. Our mouths wanted to swallow each other up. She moved her soft hand inside my briefs. Her touch drove me crazy. I kissed the tops of her breasts and unsnapped her bra. I slid it off her shoulders and let it drop to the floor. I nibbled on her nipples. She quickly unbuttoned my shirt and ripped it off my shoulders. She lowered her jeans and white panties simultaneously, while I managed to get my trousers and briefs off. We fell onto the bed. My erection was screaming and knocking at her pubic area, our lips and tongues cemented to each other, when a piercing knock entered our ears.

Before either of us could move, the second knock rattled our ears. I felt Jo's body stiffen. I sprang from the bed and tried to get my trousers on. Jo jumped up and grabbed her clothes, running to the bathroom. I managed to slip on my trousers, leaving the shirt outside my trousers to hide any bulge that wasn't going away. The third and fourth knocks came in rapid succession. Before I managed to reach the French door handle with my trembling hand, three more knocks had echoed in my ears.

Chapter 33
THE LADY IN RED

A stone faced lady, wearing a red jacket, with short black hair melted to her scalp, stood in the doorway. She carried a small, brown handbag. "I'm sorry, but we were asleep. Please come in," I said, knowing my face was still flushed from the sexual encounter, not three minutes ago. The bulge in my pants disappeared instantly once my eyes fixed on her face.

She walked into the room with authority. Her shoulders straight, head back and her heels dug into the carpeted floor as she moved across the room. She opened her handbag and pulled out a cloth measuring tape, along with a note pad and pen. "My name is Rene. I need your measurements." Her head spun around the room. "Where is the other person?" Her voice matched her face—hard, colorless, and expressionless.

"She, she is in the bathroom." I looked in the direction of the still-closed bathroom door. "Jo, the lady is here to take our measurements." No response and no expression on Rene's face. Jo never answered.

"Raise your arms," Rene instructed me, never making eye contact. She had measured my waist before Jo entered the room. "Lower your arms." She measured my sleeve length and my chest, expanded and relaxed. She stood me against the wall and marked a spot where my head leaned against the wall. She ran her tape and wrote it down.

Jo walked over to Rene, who was measuring my inseam. Rene had her right hand in my crotch and her left hand below my ankle bone. Everything fell limp in my pants, shriveling even more when Rene's fingers touched my privates. I stood in my bare feet and glanced at Jo, who gave me a quick smile. Jo's hands were folded in front of her waist. I winked, but never smiled, as I felt Rene's eyes on me. "Stand on this tape, right leg first," Rene ordered, as she knelt on the floor. She wrote the size down in the note pad and measured my other foot. She measured the width of each foot, noting them as well. Rene stood and wrapped the tape around my neck. Her fingers were ice cold, just like her face. She then ran the tape across my shoulders, writing down the number on the pad.

"Okay, lady, you're next." Her eyes gazed downward at the floor as she spoke. I stepped back and Rene began to measure Jo. She needed to measure Jo's breasts. "Take off your blouse." Jo responded by quickly unbuttoning her blouse. She raised her arms out to her side. "Stand up straight," Rene said, as she reached around Jo's breasts, holding the tape across her nipples. "What's your cup size?"

"C," Jo said, dropping her arms to her side and slipping her blouse back on. Rene finished measuring Jo and packed her things into her handbag.

"I will be back tomorrow at the same time with your clothes and everything else you will need. You must have all your personal belongings together, except for what you are wearing. The clothes you are wearing tomorrow will also be taken. You will change into the new clothes while I wait." She pulled her note pad out of her handbag and wrote down some other information. It was probably hair color, eye color and any other features. "Do any of you have any birth marks, scars or tattoos?" Rene asked. Jo and I shook our heads. "Do you have your own teeth?" We both nodded. "What about pacemaker or surgical procedures requiring artificial parts?" Jo and I both shook our heads. She looked at our fingers and toes to make sure there weren't any missing. "You ever been pregnant, miss?" Jo shook her head. Rene tossed the note pad and pen in her handbag and picked up a camera. "Okay, miss, you stand over by the wall. I need your picture for your driver's license." She took my picture right after Jo's and then headed for the door. No one spoke another word.

When the large metal door shut against the metal door jam, the ringing in our ears told us we were alone and safe at least for another day. We hoped, anyway.

Chapter 34
OCTOBER–
LANGLEY, VIRGINIA

John Conrad slammed the phone down on the solid, cherry desk he sat behind. With his palms against the edge of the desk, he pushed himself away in his high-back, black, leather chair, raising himself out of his seat. His heart rate had reached 140 beats per minute. The rage in his veins, if not controlled soon, would burst. His blood would cover every wall in this mammoth office, which overlooked the Potomac River. Conrad took a deep breath. He felt his face flush. His doctor had informed him last week his blood pressure had risen drastically, so they increased the dosage of Norvasc.

The chair he'd been sitting in slammed against the window casing, as Conrad raced toward the closed, solid, mahogany door. He opened the door, slamming it shut behind him and raced down the hall toward Travis Shear's office. With every step, he felt his chest swell.

John Conrad, fifty-eight, with thinning gray hair and a trim build, stood six feet three and wore contact lenses. Mr. Conrad joined the CIA, or Central Intelligence Agency, twenty eight years ago last month. He plans to retire in twenty three months and ten days from today.

Mr. Conrad, director of the CIA, runs a tight ship, with zero tolerance from any of its members since the many debacles of the past. He has held this position for three years. A far cry from the Company's past encounters. Mr. Conrad had been a Captain in the United States Air Force before joining the CIA. A family man, he has three daughters attending Ivy League schools. He is a member of the Methodist Church in Arlington, Virginia, where he resides with his wife, Carol.

Travis Shear sat in his office, which is half the size of Conrad's, with his feet on top of his cherry desk, talking on his cell phone to his mistress, Barbra. He'd been having an affair with her for three years. Barbra is twenty four and works for a travel agency in Arlington, Virginia. Shear is married with three children and also lives in Arlington. Shear, at six feet three inches, weighs a few pounds more and is nineteen years younger than Conrad. Travis Shear spent eight years in the United States Air Force before joining the CIA. His father, a US Senator for many years, helped him get appointed to the Air Force Academy in Colorado Springs, Colorado. Travis had been a pilot and flew sorties with Randy Abbott, Sam Abbott's brother, during the Saudi War.

Travis sat with eyes closed, about to explode from the phone sex he was having with his mistress, when Conrad flung open the door with so much force it slammed against the wall, jarring the hanging pictures. Travis's eyes flew open on the bang. Conrad, in a rage, forgot to close the door. He turned quickly and, with his right hand, grabbed the door and slammed it against the door jam, rattling the entire wall a second time. Conrad's chest tightened with every breath.

Travis dropped the phone, mouth agape, with his heart pounding faster than Conrad's. Shear's size thirteen shoes hit the carpeted floor, flinging his head forward. Shear's eyes looked like two blue saucers; his trembling hands lay on top of the desk. Realizing the cell phone he'd been talking on had dropped to the floor under his desk and he hadn't shut it off, Travis, thinking security, bent down to grab the phone with his right hand. Lifting his body before he should, he cracked his head on the desk drawer. He shut the phone off before Conrad blasted him, verbally. The stars in his eyes bounced off of Conrad's face. Travis placed the phone on the desk.

"What in God's name have you done, Shear? I just got off the phone with Jim Kelly." Jim Kelly is the director of the FBI. "Damn it, Shear, if you have anything to do with this SAWWS catastrophe, I-I will see to it, personally, you fry in hell." Conrad's face went from red to white. "Who the hell is behind this mass murder? My God, Travis. Travis, why?" Conrad took several deep breaths as his hands clutched his chest. "Oh GOD," he cried. He winced and collapsed to the floor in front of Travis's desk. Travis quickly got up and went to the aide of his chief. Travis put two fingers on the left side of Conrad's neck. No pulse. No pulse. Travis rolled him over and started pushing on his chest, counting to thirty. After ten pushes, Travis realized he should've called 911 first. After reaching 911, Travis continued pushing and counting. NO RESPONSE!

Two paramedics arrived within twenty minutes of the 911 call. They checked Conrad's vitals. The skinny one said, "We'll take him to the hospital, but this guy is dead." Travis nodded and sank into his desk chair. He looked down and a small wet spot lay on his tan slacks just to the left of his pant zipper. Travis shook his head.

Chapter 35
ON THE HOT SEAT

S econds after Conrad's body was removed, Travis's office filled with several members of the CIA wondering why, and how, their leader could have died so suddenly. Jim Brewer, the number two man in the CIA, directed all questions to Travis. Jim Brewer, forty-nine, has been in the CIA for fifteen years. He served as an Army Colonel before joining the CIA. Brewer would command the CIA, until the President of the United States appointed someone else, or elected Brewer to the post. The Senate must put their stamp of approval on whomever the President selects. Travis attempted to answer all the questions as best he could. In most cases, one word answers were given. Brewer asked all the other members to leave the office. Brewer stood looking out the window. Travis remained slumped in his leather chair. "Travis, why was John so mad? What the hell happened this morning to trigger John's rage?" Brewer's voice remained calm, yet crisp. Brewer had heard the door-slamming earlier. In fifteen years, he had never seen Conrad slam anything.

Travis felt a cold shiver climb over his skin. His stomach now climbed towards his throat. Thoughts of his family entered his head, along with thoughts of Barbra. Travis knew something went bad, really bad with project, **"Underground"**. Several seconds elapsed while Travis deciphered the past six months.

Brewer, with his hands planted on the front of Travis's desk and staring holes through Travis's eyes said, "Travis, answer the damn questions."

Travis never looked at Brewer. "I-I don't know."

"You bastard, Shear, I've never liked your sorry ass since you became a member of the CIA. The only reason you're here is because of your goddamn corrupt father." The veins in Brewer's neck came alive as he spoke. "I don't trust you or your father. Your father has the CIA's hands tied and you know it. But when I get to the bottom of this, and I will, you'll wish you never had your daddy get you a job here." Brewer's eyes stayed on Travis for a good minute. "Remember, asshole, I'm not afraid of you or your father." Jim Brewer turned slowly and left the office, leaving Shear sitting in his chair. Travis stared into the past several months with the pit of his stomach on fire.

Chapter 36
THIRTY
MINUTES LATER

Travis Shear tried to digest what had just happened. His head pounded; mouth parched. He needed to leave the office and see his daddy. Daddy would have the answers to these questions that were stirring around in his head. Travis was scared.

It took Travis thirty minutes to drive to Senator Shear's office. Travis walked past Rachael's, Sterling's secretary, desk and barged into his father's office. He found Rhonda on her knees in front of Sterling, while he slouched, eyes closed, on his leather sofa. Travis did an about face and headed toward the closed door. Travis left. Rhonda and Sterling never knew he had entered the office.

Rhonda left out the back door and Rachael called the Senator's desk. "Yeah, Rachael, what is it?" the Senator said, standing in front of the mirror, straightening his tie and making sure his perfectly styled hair was not out of place.

"Senator, I have your son out here." Rachael paused a few seconds. "Would you like for me to send him in?"

"Yes, Rachael, send him in." Sterling took a hanky from his rear pants pocket and wiped the remaining sweat off his forehead.

Travis walked into his father's office with weak legs, dry mouth, and a lump in his stomach. "Father, we have serious problems."

The Senator looked at him with puzzled eyes and leaned back in his chair. "What kind of problems do you have?"

"Conrad died in my office less than two hours ago. He had gotten a call from Kelly and he wanted to know what the hell I had to do with SAWWS Inc."

"What did you tell him?" Shear asked quickly, leaning on his desk with his forearms.

"I said nothing," Travis answered, as he paced the floor.

"So, don't worry about it."

"You don't get it father. Kelly knows who did it. I need to get the hell out of the country." Travis headed toward the window.

"Are you sure Kelly knows, or are they bluffing?"

"Believe me, they know."

"What the hell went wrong?" Sterling stood.

"I don't know father."

"What the hell? What do you mean you don't know?" Sterling's face turned bright red.

Travis remained quiet for several minutes, pondering what to say or do. He has always been afraid of his father since he was a little kid. His father would lose his temper and throw things and beat on him until he was black and blue. Several times Travis had to be taken to the hospital. Sterling had broken Travis's arm once and his nose three times. He also had been knocked unconscious several times.

Travis had learned from his Aunt Rita, his mother's sister, that his grandfather, his father's father, Peyton Shear, had beaten up Sterling when he was a kid. The Senator would take his frustrations out on Travis. Afterwards, he would buy expensive things for Travis, or take him to places like Disneyland, or exotic beaches. The beatings stopped when Travis entered the Air Force Academy. Travis has never touched his children in any harmful way.

"Travis, speak to me, damn it." Sterling stood inches away from his son.

Travis's eyes watered; his lips munched together; his hands clammy. "I hav-I haven't talked to anyone since October 12th." Travis's eyes looked down at the plush carpeted floor to his right.

"Travis, you have your mother's spine and her brains. If this operation in any way leads to me, I will personally see to it that you rot in hell." Sterling pointed his right index finger in front of Travis's nose. "You bastards were supposed to kill and destroy all of SAWWS Inc. employees, including Abbott and his wife." Sterling's eyes widened— widened as in scary. "Now, what the hell happened? I paid you sons- of-bitches a lot of money to get the job done and it was supposed to be done right," Sterling screamed.

"I-I don-I don't know."

"Get out of my office and find out. I want answers, boy, and I want them fast. Do you hear me or do I have to draw you a map?" The Senator picked up a $2500 bronze statue from an end table and fired it across the room, striking the walled book shelves. Books and parts of the cherry bookcase scattered everywhere upon contact. Sterling turned around and screamed vulgarities at his son until he left his office.

Chapter 37

THE FBI IS HERE

Two hours later Senator Shear plopped into the leather chair behind his desk and put his hands over his face. The phone rang. He jumped. His hands fell to the desk. He stared at the phone. It rang three more times before Shear pushed the speaker phone button. "Yeah, Rachael!" Shear spoke with a dying breath.

"I have Jim Kelly, Director of the FBI, here to see you." Rachael paused. "He says it is urgent."

Shear's heart tightened quickly. His stomach froze and dryness struck his throat. Thoughts slammed into his head like two trains hitting head on. An explosion hammered between his ears. He looked out the window and wanted to run. He and Rhonda could escape to some small island in the Pacific. "Ah, Rachael, ah, send him in." His voice trailed off.

Director Kelly stood six feet three inches and weighed 210 pounds. At forty-nine, he had a body of a professional athlete. He'd been appointed Director of the FBI five years ago by the previous President. Shear didn't fear any man, except Kelly. Kelly didn't fear anyone, not even the President of the United States. Kelly has been with the FBI for twenty one years. He has an impeccable record. He is married and has two sons in college.

The door to the Senator's office opened and in walked Kelly, along with two FBI agents. Kelly wore a navy blue, two piece suit. His hair showed some graying around his temples. The other two members of the FBI were also dressed in two piece suits similar to Kelly's. Shear knew if he tried to stand up, his legs would buckle. He stayed put. He made eye contact with Kelly and then dropped them to his cluttered desk. Looking down, he noticed his still-opened fly from the encounter with Rhonda. He quickly zipped it up and continued to stare at his desk.

"Senator, this is Agent Becker and Agent Stanton. We are here to inform you we have proof you and your son, Travis, along with several of his CIA buddies, are responsible for the massacre of the people at SAWWS Inc. Your son and ten of his buddies at the CIA have already been apprehended and are in our custody. We also have the Presidents and CEOs of three drug companies, along with the officers of Mallory, Pittman, and Herrington, in custody." Agent Becker pulled handcuffs from his coat pocket. "You have the right to remain silent. Anything you say may be used against you in a court of law." Shear never moved; his body paralyzed; his eyes glazed. "Stand up, Shear. We are going to take you to 935 Pennsylvania Ave." The J. Edgar Hoover Building, FBI headquarters, sits at this address. The FBI has occupied this building since June 1977. The building has over 2,800,000 square feet of floor space for over 7000 employees. The FBI has an annual budget of over 3.8 billion dollars, with an additional 28,800 employees scattered all over the world.

Shear never moved, so Agents Becker and Stanton pulled his limp body out of his custom built, leather chair. "Shear you can walk out of here with or without cuffs. If we walk out of here without cuffs and you cause any disturbance whatsoever, we will not hesitate to make a scene in front of the public and many of your constituents." Shear stared at the floor, saying nothing. "Did I make my self clear, Senator?" Kelly barked. Shear nodded. It was the first time Shear moved a muscle or did anything since the FBI interrupted his life.

The four men walked out of Shear's office. "Rachael, hold all my appointments for the rest of the week." Shear spoke in a very slow, soft tone, without making any eye contact with his secretary. Rachael sat there with her mouth wide open.

The four men entered a dark blue Lincoln Navigator. Kelly and Shear sat in the back seat and Becker and Stanton in the front, with Becker driving. They arrived at 935 Pennsylvania Ave in the underground parking garage. Kelly, Becker and Stanton escorted the Senator to the third floor. Shear never said a word.

After being fingerprinted and strip searched, Shear was led to an office, where he had access to a phone, paper, pen, and an empty glass with a pitcher of ice water next to it. "You can make several phone calls, Senator. I would advise you to call your attorney first because you're not getting out of here on any bail. We already have enough on you and the rest of your team to put you in prison and, possibly, get the death penalty." Jim Kelly's facial expression stayed hard and his eyes fixed on Shear's startled face as he spoke. Shear stared back. His eyes sank into his head.

"I want some privacy." Shear spoke firmly, but again his words trailed off.

"Okay, Senator. You have thirty minutes to make those phone calls. Enjoy them because it will be a cold, very cold, day before you get to use another phone."

The time was 1538 when he dialed the President's oval office. Shear had the number of the President's direct line stored in his head. The phone rang five times before the President answered with a hurried and out of breath response. "This is the President." The President had been engaged in intercourse with one of Shear's escort ladies, Brandi, when the phone rang.

"Tony, this is Shear!"

"Yes, Senator Shear. How are ya doing?" The President had a big shit-eatin' grin on his face.

"Not good, Mr. President!" Shear's voice cracked on each word.

"What's the problem?" The President stood naked by his desk with Brandi next to him.

"The FBI has my ass down here at the Hoover building on charges of being the brains behind the SAWWS Inc. killings." Shear's forehead and armpits were wet with perspiration.

"Sterling, I'm sure you didn't have anything to do with that." The President looked at Brandi.

"Absolutely not, this is totally absurd. I have an impeccable record. I need for you to call Kelly and get my ass out of here. I have a dinner party this evening."

"I'll get right on it, Shear."

"Thanks. I owe you."

"Okay, Senator!" The President dropped the phone on the desk before he reached for the arms on his chair. He became blurry-eyed and collapsed in a heap on the floor. Brandi screamed at the top of her lungs, bringing the secret service men running.

Hysterical, Brandi was about to go into shock when the secret service men entered the oval office. Briefly glancing at the naked escort lady, they went directly to the aide of the President. Agent Small touched the artery on the President's neck and found a pulse. "He's alive! Call Rosie. We need to get him to the hospital." Rosie was the dispatcher for the

Secret Service that day. The President, however, lay motionless, with his eyes closed. Agent Brown said, "He must have had a heart attack when he was having sex with what's her face."

A helicopter transported the President to Walter Reed Hospital, where he was rushed into intensive care. Within two hours, the President was sitting up and talking with three doctors. The President suffered from low sugar and needed to eat regularly. His sexual encounter with Brandi, combined with not having eaten any lunch due to having to attend meetings with Iran's and Iraq's foreign ambassadors, caused his blood sugar to drop.

The President rode back to the oval office by helicopter. He entered his office and had a message to call Senator Shear at the FBI headquarters. "Oh, shit! I have to call Kelly!"

"Jim, this is the President!" Kelly twisted his mouth in disgust.

"Yes, Mr. President what can I do for you?" Kelly made a fist.

"Say, Jim, I need for you to release Senator Shear. There has to be some sort of mistake."

"No mistake, Mr. President! He is as guilty as I'm sitting here talking to you."

The President paused several seconds. "We have to keep this under wraps. We must not have the media find out. Christ almighty, it will bury this country if they found out Shear was behind this."

"I have officers from three drug companies, ten CIA agents, Travis Shear, the Senator's son, and six officers of the Mallory, Pittman and Herrington law firm from New York City, who represent the drug companies. Shear is the brains behind the massacre. He was paid a billion dollars by the drug companies to destroy SAWWS Inc. Murdering all these people was their only means to end SAWWS Inc. manufacturing. I have signed confessions from twelve people already."

"Kelly, I don't give a damn what you have or how you got it. I don't want the media or anyone else finding out a damn thing. This country will absolutely shit if they know Shear and members of the CIA are involved. Jesus Christ, if this isn't a mess. Abbott is still alive, isn't he?" The President stalled before he spoke again. "I want you and Jim Brewer in my office in one hour. Is that understood?"

"Yes, Sir!" Kelly responded, as his jaw tightened.

The President called Brewer's office immediately after hanging up with Kelly.

Chapter 38
MEETING WITH THE PRESIDENT

Jim Kelly was the first person to reach the oval office. The President's secretary, Sandy, had him wait until Jim Brewer from the CIA arrived. Jim got there eighteen minutes later.

Ten minutes after both men had met outside the President's oval office, Sandy's phone beeped. "Yes, Mr. President." She tried to smile, but failed. "Mr. Kelly and Mr. Brewer, you may step into the oval office."

Both Brewer and Kelly smiled and entered the office. They sat in front of the President's desk in two ornate cherry chairs. "Okay, I want to hear everything you have—from the beginning."

Brewer told his story about the Director of the CIA, John Conrad. After sharing this information with Jim Kelly, Kelly then ordered his agents to investigate the disappearance of the employees of SAWWS Inc. After both men had finished, the President appeared shocked. He slumped back in his chair, looked at both men, and sprang forward, laying his arms on his desk.

"We have one hell of a problem here." The President pondered for a minute, rubbing his hands and playing with some papers on his desk. "We must not, in any way, let this information leak to anyone, especially the media. Why, if the media caught wind of this, the American people would go crazy. We have here three of the biggest drug companies, the CIA and a prominent Senator involved. Shear has done more for this country than all the other Senators combined. He has taken the poorest State in the union, Mississippi, and turned it into one of the union's strongest States, not only economically, but educationally as well. He has done wonders. People, black and white, worship this man, not only in Mississippi, but across this fine nation of ours."

The President got up and walked around the oval office. "Just think about all the wonderful people who take drugs from these drug companies. If they find out, it will ruin this nation." He spun around. Wringing his moist hands, he continued. "This will destroy, destroy this ____." The President sat down in his chair, quickly, and thought for a few seconds about: If the media were to print any of this—the two hour sex marathon he had had with Brandi earlier that day. His stomach lay in the devil's fire. He needed a drink—NOW. He wiped his red face with his sweaty hand and blurted out, with his finger pointed at both Kelly and Brewer, "You make damn sure this never reaches the media." The President then collapsed back in his chair; his face turned ashen.

Jim Kelly's lips moved as he stirred in his ornate char, but no sound came out. Finally, when the President stopped, he opened up. "Mr. President, your great Senator, Sterling Shear, was not only the brains, but the financial strength behind this massacre. He also is and has been for many, many years a large financial supporter of the Klu Klux Klan in Mississippi."

"But, he has helped more blacks in this country than anybody, including the damn NAACP," said the President, his eyes widening like saucers, voice cracking on each word. The President's mouth fell open and his fingers on his right hand covered his opened mouth. He was aghast.

"The great Senator Shear has over five hundred million dollars that we know about, in European banks, most of which in Swiss banks. We are still digging, Mr. President, and have been for several months."

"You can chalk up another useless death because of that Goddamn Shear," barked, Jim Brewer. "John Conrad would be here today if it weren't for this rotten son-of-a-bitch. I want this bastard to fry and I want the public to know what a corrupt weasel he is. He has everyone snowed, especially those in the State of Mississippi. I hate it that eleven of my men were involved in this brutal crime. Money and sex talk, Mr. President. This is how Shear has gained his popularity, success, and made his money."

"I'm sorry, gentlemen! I don't want Senator Shear prosecuted for these murders. I want him released from your office immediately. This will have to cool down and that may take months. I will talk to Senator Shear, personally. He will be asked to resign his Senate seat due to poor health. We will move his ass to maybe some third world country and the media will print that he died a horrible death from cancer. I don't want any person you have in custody brought to justice. I want these people destroyed and Brewer, you have ways of doing that." The President spoke with slobber rolling off his lips.

Brewer stood up quickly and replied, "I will not destroy these men. They will be brought to trial. That is the American way. If you stand in my way, I will turn in my resignation right now. I want to run a tight ship, just as John Conrad had done for the years he was Director."

"I can replace you right now, Brewer. I'm the President and I'll tell you when, where and how much, anytime I wish. Do you understand that?" The President's face turned red as a ripe tomato.

Brewer thought about his kids in college and having very little money in savings due to his wife's spending sprees. "Yes, Sir, I understand that. But, do you understand what will happen if the media ever gets hold of any inkling that you knew about Shear and you let him walk?"

Brewer walked across the floor of the oval office. "Furthermore, Mr. President, did you know that Shear has more call girls on his payroll than there are nuns in D.C.?"

"Between Kelly and me, we have enough to put Shear away for a thousand years."

"I don't care. I want him moved to a third world country next month and send that slut, Rhonda Jones, with him." The President had first-hand knowledge of Ms. Jones.

"Are you going to let Shear keep all his money?" Brewer shot back.

"Yes! Why not? It's his money, regardless of how he earned it."

"Several hundred million would help a lot of young people further their education," Kelly chimed in.

"I had to earn my money to go to school. They can, too."

"How soon do you want this asshole sent away?" Brewer asked.

"Give Sterling a month to be diagnosed with some sort of terminal cancer." The President shuffled papers on his desk and then laid them back down again.

"What are we going to do with the others?" Brewer asked.

"Shoot them, drown them, run over them, I don't give a damn. Just eliminate them."

"What are you going to do about SAWWS Inc.?" Kelly asked.

"Where is Abbott? Why haven't you found him? You need to find him before he causes us problems." The President's face was in stroke readiness. His blood pressure far exceeded its limits, even with medication. He opened his desk drawer and grabbed the bottle of blood pressure pills, putting a tablet in his mouth. He managed to swallow it without any water.

"We have some good leads, but we now know he is innocent," Kelly said.

"Innocent, or not, I want him out of the picture. With him around, the lid is still open. I want the lid slammed shut, ASAP. Is that clear gentlemen? I want Abbott dead before the end of the week," the President shouted.

"Yes, it is clear, Mr. President!" Brewer said. Kelly nodded. They both rose from their ornate chairs and walked toward the door.

Before leaving, Kelly turned and said, "You never mentioned what you wanted done with SAWWS Inc."

"I don't know. Just leave it alone," the President responded as sweat dripped from his face.

Brewer and Kelly left the oval office. The President's thoughts were spinning around in his head: If Shear is prosecuted, he will drag many senators, congressmen and me into his web. We would all go down the drain. He must be destroyed, along with Abbott.

Chapter 39
THE JOURNEY

We left the hotel with all bills paid, a different car, new names, new clothes, a credit card, new driver licenses, and directions to someplace neither of us had ever been to before. All my employees were confirmed dead, either poisoned by toxic gases or brutally beaten and dismembered, with Jennifer being the only one identified by DNA. Right now, my body is running on hate, revenge, and unanswered questions as to who is responsible. Jo seemed to be on the verge of a mental breakdown. We can't go to any doctors or pharmacies for fear of being caught. We will be staying with people we never met. We wondered every second when we might be stopped by the law, or if we will be on the run forever.

We drove down I-55 from Chicago toward St Louis, Missouri. It's 10:55 am and ten days have passed since I had talked to Jennifer and Virginia. Now, they are dead. I am on the run and trying to keep my body from exploding into a million pieces. The buildup inside me makes me nauseous; my head pounds at my temples. The tightness in my neck and shoulders causes numbness down to my fingertips and scrambled thoughts. I have trouble breathing. I flipped on the A/C to cool me down. We have been on this road for two hours and just passed Bloomington, Illinois' last exit.

The telephone poles fly by; cars and trucks pass us. We were told to stay under the posted speed limit of 70 mph. I looked down at the speedometer and it read 66 mph. My hands gripped the wheel so tightly my knuckles turned white. I tried to relax, but thoughts ran through my head faster than the speed of sound. I looked straight ahead and saw red lights flashing on our side of the road. Traffic slowed. Jo had her eyes shut, possibly asleep. It looked like a road block. "Shit!" I tapped the brake pedal to slow my momentum until we were under 25mph. Jo's eyes remained closed. "What now?" I tried to peer over the cars in front of me to see what was happening. Before I knew why or what, a large lawman dressed in an Illinois State Trooper uniform flagged me down. He motioned me over to the shoulder, where several cars were parked in various directions. I was petrified. Jo awoke, saw the flashing lights and screamed—screams filled with panic, fright, and pent-up emotion. The trooper looked in my side window. He drew his gun, as did three other troopers. Traffic was now stopped. Four more troopers arrived on the scene and circled our car. "Shit! David, where are you? I need you David." Jo was hysterical. I laid my hand on her left thigh, trying to slow the madness escaping from within her trembling body.

"Unlock your doors!" shouted the largest trooper, standing a few feet from my door.

I fumbled with the locks on the door panel, unlocking them, locking them and finally, unlocking them. Two troopers flung open both the driver's door and the front passenger's door, simultaneously. "GET OUT WITH YOUR HANDS UP!"

I tried to move, but my seat belt clamped me to my seat. Jo had gone into shock or had passed out from fright. My body stiffened. My hands were cold. My eyes saw Jennifer in front of the car. She smiled and then put an elbow of her sunglasses between her lips. My eyes watered. I closed them and opened them, but she was still there.

My eyes burned from tears, tears of joy. Just then, large hands gripped my shirt at my shoulder and drug me out of the car. I was still focused on Jennifer, as my knees slammed onto the cement pavement. The pain shot up to my shoulders. I felt a large knee press hard between my shoulder blades, slamming my face onto the highway. Jennifer was still smiling.

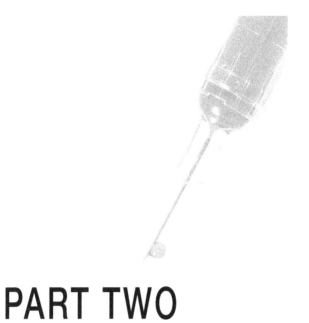

PART TWO

Chapter 40
NEW ZEALAND

I woke up with a cold sweat oozing from my naked body, in a bed with a body lying next to me. My palms were clammy. My eyes opened wide, staring at a ceiling not familiar to me. The body lying next to me was covered and faced the other way. The room was bright enough to see, even though there were no lights on, just a ray of light from outside seeping through the drapes. It looked like Jennifer's hair. I sat up immediately and put my right hand on the body. My heart was ready to jump out from under my rib cage after hearing the body moan. "It's alive," I whispered. Seconds later the body moved, turning on its back to give me a full view of her face. It was Jennifer. "OH, MY GOD!" I blinked. It was a dream. No, it was a damn nightmare, a nightmare from hell. I shook, tears ran down my cheeks and I couldn't move. I shook my head trying to clear the insanity of my nightmare.

I glanced at the clock on the night stand and read the illuminated red numbers facing me: 3:45 am. Where am I? I looked around the room and then it struck me—is this our room in Auckland, New Zealand? Should I tell Jennifer? Should I make sure and peak outside the curtains. I gently walked to the window with legs like straw, so weak I could barely move. I looked down at the street lights below watching a few cars and trucks going down the wrong side of the road. I must be in New Zealand.

I turned away from the window and looked at Jennifer lying in the bed, breathing in rhythm. I was stunned, paralyzed, and could hardly breathe. My chest tightened; my mouth parched. I went to the bathroom and ran cold water from the tap into a glass I had taken from the vanity. I gulped it down and ran another glassful, and another, until my mouth had enough saliva to move my tongue. I glanced in the mirror after turning on the light switch, and saw Sam Abbott. The real Sam Abbott, not Trevor. "Jo, OH MY GOD! Who! Why! How!" Her partially naked body entered my head. I turned abruptly, looking back at Jennifer. "I won't tell Jennifer about my nightmare. It isn't necessary! I want to forget it. I hope I can forget it." I looked back at the mirror to make sure I saw Sam.

I walked back to the bed where Jennifer, half uncovered, lay on her back, with her arms by her side. I headed toward the bed and gently pulled the covers off, exposing the rest of her luscious body. I leaned down and kissed her gently on the forehead, her left cheek, her breasts, and her stomach. Within minutes, she lost control and so had I, until an hour had passed.

Exhausted, we wrapped our arms around each other. She fell asleep quickly, while I lay awake, still making sure she did not leave, nor will never, ever leave, my side. Never again.

Chapter 41
THIRD DAY IN NEW ZEALAND

It was our third morning waking up in Auckland, New Zealand. We had no plans; we were playing it by ear. We made love three and four times each day, eating in the room with no clothes on. We were reliving the days ten years ago when we had first met in Taupo. I still had memories of my nightmare rattling around inside my head. I hadn't read a paper or even looked at the TV, except when we rented a movie to watch in our room. I had not spoken to Virginia since we had left.

We dressed, figuring we ought to get some fresh air. We headed downtown toward the marina. We walked around for more than an hour before settling on the Belini Bar, which faced the marina. I drank a Dewar's on the rocks and Jennifer had a fancy cream drink with three different white liquors in it. After several hours and three drinks apiece, we were feeling good and thought it best to get a bite to eat. We chose the White Restaurant not too far from the Belini Bar. We were somewhat tipsy from the drinks we had had at Belini's.

Jennifer headed to the restroom to freshen up, as I ordered a bottle of New Zealand wine. I ordered a 2006 Palliser Estate Martin Sauvignon Blanc, one of the finest wines of New Zealand. Twenty minutes had gone by since Jennifer had left for the powder room. I had already consumed half of my glass. I was feeling no pain, with millions in the bank, a multi-million dollar enterprise which had endless earnings, and a beautiful wife I will cherish for the rest of my life. "Where is she? It has been almost a half hour now?" After five more minutes, I got up and headed toward the powder room. I asked a young, attractive, Kiwi girl to go in the powder room and check if my wife was okay. She came back out and informed me she wasn't in there. I blurted out, with a half- paralyzed tongue, "She has to be in there." Memories of my nightmare plowed furrows through my head.

"I'm afraid not, sir. There is no one in the powder room. I even looked in all the stalls." She smiled and walked away, leaving me in a non-sober state. Thoughts of the tunnel, the gas in the tunnel, filled my head.

I headed back to our table, bumping into chairs along the way. Alcohol was entering my blood stream too fast and my wife was missing. "I'm not dreaming this. It is real, isn't it?" I sat down, trying to gather my thoughts and trying to keep the marbles from rattling around inside my head. I took another large swallow of wine and managed to stand and walk outside to get a bit of fresh air. The couple of minutes of fresh air I took in rejuvenated my brain enough to gather my senses. I went back inside and asked for the maitre d, Mr. Killion, a balding, middle-aged man. "Mr. Killion, my wife is missing from your restaurant. She went to the powder room 45 minutes ago and she isn't in the powder room and she isn't in your restaurant. Can you call the police?"

"Mr. Abbott, I will notify the police, immediately. Please, wait over there and they will be here very shortly." He pointed toward an ornate piece of furniture Jennifer and I had sat in before being seated at our table.

Several long minutes later, two unarmed, uniformed police came through the front door. New Zealand's police officers don't pack a firearm. They do, however, pack a friendly smile and a warm, sincere, understanding mannerism. I explained my dilemma to the two officers, Ruskin and Cambridge. They informed me that over 8000 missing person claims are filed each year in New Zealand, with over 95 % of them located within a few days. "Mr. Abbott, do you happen to have a picture of Mrs. Abbott on you?" asked Officer Ruskin, the taller of the two officers.

I reached for my wallet and tried quickly to fetch the picture of Jennifer. I handed it to Officer Cambridge. "A very attractive lady, Mr. Abbott. We should be able to locate her very quickly. Our officers are well trained and we have the latest scientific equipment to handle these types of cases." He smiled at the picture, as if he liked her in a sensual way. "What is her first name, Mr. Abbott?"

"We are staying at the Langham Hotel," I said, with perspiration running down the small of my back. "That picture is about a year old. Her first name is Jennifer, spelled J-E-N-N-I-F-E-R." I managed to spit out.

"Mr. Abbott, can you tell us what your wife is wearing, color of her hair and anything else we might need to know about her?" He had his paper and pen ready to take notes.

"Yes, she is wearing a pair of Capri pants. Ah, let's see. Yes, they are plaid, various colors. I would say blue, green, and maybe cream or beige and they had a belt, a green belt. She had on a light blue top with sleeves, short sleeves, and a pair of earrings; they were small gold earrings, I believe, yes, gold," I said, with my eyes dancing from Cambridge to Ruskin.

"What about a watch, shoes, her hair, and any tattoos?" asked Officer Cambridge.

"Her shoes were slip-ons, toeless. I can't remember the color of them, maybe a light green. I'm not sure," I said, with sweat still running down my back.

"Tattoos, Mr. Abbott?" Cambridge asked, staring into my wet, bloodshot eyes.

"No, no tattoos. She didn't like them. In fact, she thought they were hideous, especially on women."

"Mr. Abbott, what about a watch, any rings?" Ruskin asked, with Cambridge waiting to take the information down.

"Yes, she had on an inexpensive watch. I believe it was a Swiss manufacturer. It had been her grandmother's, just a plain watch, with no diamonds or anything." I can't believe this is happening as I peer around, trying to see if Jennifer is anywhere. My nightmare is now rambling through my head like it was all real. Am I going crazy?

"Any rings on Mrs. Abbott's fingers?" asked Officer Ruskin.

"Oh, yes. She has a large, three-carat, diamond ring, plus a wedding band."

"Is the ring silver or gold?" Cambridge asked.

"Silver, I think. Yeah, silver." My head is real foggy.

"What about her hair, Mr. Abbott?" Ruskin asked, as he pulled on his ear.

I looked at both officers and tried to think, as the booze ran rapidly through my veins. "Her hair is short. It is a dark color, her natural color, almost black. She just got her hair cut before we left Georgia. It comes down to about here." I put my hand on my neck, showing the two officers.

"Any scars on Mrs. Abbott?" Cambridge asked, with his pen ready to record my response.

"No scars. Wait, she does have a scar on her left knee, where she had surgery from a skiing accident many years ago." The deli where we had met ten years ago popped into my head. "The scar is faint. The surgeon did a great job."

"Any birthmarks?" Ruskin asked, glancing at a lady walking across the floor, who resembled Jennifer.

I quickly saw who Ruskin was looking at and said, "Jennifer." The lady never turned around, just kept walking. She wore Capri pants, slip-on shoes and had short, black hair. I moved quickly toward the lady and hollered her name again. "JENNIFER" My mouth felt like cement dust. She never even glanced at me. I moved back toward the officers.

"Mr. Abbott, about any birthmarks on Mrs. Abbott," Cambridge asked.

"What, what did you ask?" I felt sick inside. The scotch I had drunk earlier floated to my throat.

"Birthmarks, any birthmarks on Mrs. Abbott?" Cambridge repeated.

"No! No, she doesn't have any birthmarks." I felt like throwing up.

"Mr. Abbott, do you want to sit down? You don't look too good," Officer Ruskin said, taking my arm and moving me toward a chair.

"No, I'm okay! I just want this nightmare to end."

Immediately, a puzzled look came over both Officers. Cambridge asked, after I sat down, "You said a nightmare. Are you telling us about a nightmare, or is your wife actually missing?"

I looked at them both with puzzlement filtering out of my eyes. I'm going crazy. No, I can't be. Jo stood in front of me. Everything went black.

Chapter 42
TWO HOURS LATER

opened my eyes, blinking several times, head splitting and my mouth as dry as desert sand. I glanced around the room and realized immediately: I'm in a hospital or some sort of medical facility. There is a needle taped into each arm and I am as naked as a plucked chicken. The bed has two side rails from my head to my cold feet. "Why are my feet cold?" It appeared to be a private room. I looked for some sort of button to push for a nurse or anyone to come in and tell me what was going on. It smelled like a hospital. "What happened? Who brought me here? Shit, I'm strapped in this damn bed." I panicked. I realized I had a tube up my nose and wires leading from my strapped body to a machine with blips dancing across a screen. "My heart rate is being monitored. I have a cuff on my right arm leading to another monitor giving my blood pressure reading, which I can't see. I know it is high. Am I having a heart attack, or did I have a heart attack?" I screamed, "JENNIFER" I waited for a few seconds. I heard nothing. "JENNIFER" I waited a few more seconds. Nothing registered in my ears, not even a tick or a tock. "NURSE, COME HERE," I hollered, breathing faster now.

I laid there for several minutes, with beads of sweat on my forehead, before a nurse, dressed all in white, came into the room. "Mr. Abbott, you're awake," she said, smiling and walking quickly toward my bed. Her flawless face glowed and her eyes looked warm.

No shit, I thought, before my mouth opened with, "Where am I? Where is my wife, my wife, Jennifer?"

"You are at Mercy Hospital. The police said you had lost your wife and then you passed out. They had the emergency people bring you here a few hours ago. We are doing some tests. The doctor will be in to see you momentarily."

"What about my wife? Have the police found my wife?" The expression on her face told me the answer to my question. My mouth opened, waiting for her to speak.

"The police are here in the lobby. I'll call them." She left the room, briskly.

"Could I have some water?" I screamed through parched lips.

A nurse's aid brought the water before the police arrived. I gulped it down, quickly, through a bent straw and asked for more. The glass was refilled from a pitcher and handed to me. Again, I slurped it down. The nurse's aide then did an about face and left the room, not saying one word.

Officers Ruskin and Cambridge entered my room shortly after the nurse's aide left. "How are you, Mr. Abbott?" Ruskin asked, with a grin which vanished with one step toward my bed. Cambridge, right behind Ruskin, said, "I hope you are feeling better Mr. Abbott." His smile also disappeared immediately after he spoke.

No good news, I thought. "Where is my wife?"

Seconds passed before Cambridge spoke. "Ah, Mr. Abbott, your wife is still missing, unfortunately. However, we have the entire New Zealand police force and security people on the look out for Mrs. Abbott. We have notified the Australian authorities also, just in case."

Ruskin chimed in seconds later with, "We have notified every airport, bus station and other modes of public transportation to be on the look out for her. We will find her, Mr. Abbott. Hopefully, we will have something in a few hours"

"What am I doing in this hospital? I have to get out of here so I can locate Jennifer."

"You passed out at the restaurant and we summoned an ambulance to bring you here," Cambridge replied.

"Why did I pass out?"

"You had a bit too much to drink and maybe not enough food. The hotel said you checked in three days ago and never left the room—until today. Is that correct Mr. Abbott?" Ruskin asked, with no doubt in his eyes.

"Yes, it's true, but we did order room service a few times."

"That is true, but you only ordered food four times and the food wasn't nearly enough for two people to function on, unless they slept the entire time. Did you and Mrs. Abbott sleep most of the time you were in the room?"

"Ah no, we—What kind of question is that officer?"

"We believe you have had very little food and consumed lots of alcohol in the past three days and, combined with the time change, this caused you to pass out at the restaurant." Ruskin then glanced at Cambridge, holding his smile briefly.

"The doctor will do an evaluation on you in a few minutes. Then, we can move on from there," Cambridge said, with a quick smile at the end.

Just then, Dr. McMillen walked into the room. "Good afternoon, Mr. Abbott. I see you are awake." He took his stethoscope from around his neck and plugged it in his ears, running the other end, a cold piece, over my bare chest. After a few coughs and the cold piece moving around my chest, the doctor said, "Your vital signs seem normal; we put you on an IV to get some nourishment in your body. Your tank was running on empty. You'll be okay. I hope the police locate your wife. I'll see the nurses. We should get you out of here within a few hours." He released my arm restraints and let the rails down on my bed, making me a free man once again.

"Why can't I leave now?" I demanded.

"You need some more fuel in your tank before we can let you go. This IV gives you more nourishment than a couple of steaks and works much faster. I suggest you go and eat a good meal and then get some sleep," Doctor McMillen advised, as he left the room.

"Mr. Abbott, have you and your wife had any marital problems? Did you two have an argument since you've been at the Langham Hotel?"

"No." My eyebrows went to the top of my head, instantly. "We have never had an argument in the ten years we've been married." Adoption of a baby popped into my head, but I never mentioned it.

"Was Mrs. Abbott upset with anything before she left for the powder room?" Ruskin asked.

"No, we were having a great time. We met ten years ago in Taupo, New Zealand." Memories of me and Jennifer running naked around the hotel room jumped into my head.

Officer Cambridge's cell phone rang. He answered, "This is Cambridge." After a minute or so, he smiled broadly, and said, "Thanks, I will tell him." He returned the cell phone to his pocket. "We have located your wife and she is okay. She became disoriented and was located wandering around the marina." I became ecstatic. "She, too, had passed out at a small park by the marina. I believe both of you have had too much alcohol and not enough sleep or food."

"When can I see her?"

"The patrolman who found her is bringing her here, shortly," Officer Cambridge said, smiling. Officer Ruskin reached over the rail of my bed, shook my hand and wished me the best of luck. They both turned and left the room, leaving me happy and wanting my wife back in my arms.

"I want some food," I blurted out, still not seeing any button to push for a nurse.

Within seconds, a nurse's aide, a cute friendly, young lady, popped into my room. "What would you like to eat?"

"I don't care, maybe a steak, baked potato and a small salad."

"We don't have any steak here at the hospital, but we can get you some fresh fruit: kiwi, grapes, oranges, mango, and pineapple. You should eat fresh fruit now that you are being fed through the IV."

"Okay, fruit it is."

Minutes after I received my fruit plate, Jennifer came running into my room. "Jennifer!" I screamed.

Chapter 43
BACK AT THE LANGHAM HOTEL

They discharged me two hours after Jennifer had arrived. We took a cab back to the Langham Hotel. We laughed and hugged one another; yet, fear ran through our veins about what could have happened. Jennifer ordered room service: Two medium rare T-Bone steaks with two baked potatoes, garden salad and assorted vegetables. No liquor. We ate slowly, savoring every bite.

After setting the empty dishes outside the door on the floor, we both stripped down and entered the shower together. For the past ten years, we have not been able to keep our hands off each other, whether naked or dressed. We were both exhausted, but the sexual energy riveted throughout our bodies. "I want you, Sam," Jennifer purred in my ear.

I want you, my love." We rinsed the soap from our wet bodies. I dried Jennifer with a large, soft bath towel and she did the same for me. We collapsed onto the bed, with the sun shining behind the drapes on the window. We were asleep within minutes and slept until awakened by loud pounding on the door.

Chapter 44
WHERE AM I?

Pitch black. I didn't know if I was blind or if it had really turned dark. My body stiffened immediately, while my eyes tried to focus on some sort of resemblance. I was on some sort of hard bed. "Jennifer?" I whispered. Lying on my right side, I slowly rolled over on my back, feeling around me for Jennifer. My body became cold, but I started to sweat; my head pounded, pounding like when I was in the tunnel. My stomach is on fire. I have to puke. Where will I puke? Too late! I upchucked for several seconds. It relieved the pounding in my head. "The tunnel, the blasted tunnel, I'm being gassed again. No! Jennifer!" I screamed. I waited for a sound, any sound, but nothing, not even the sound of my rapid breathing. Am I deaf and blind? I can still touch, but not sure if I can smell since I can't smell anything—not even my own puke.

Several minutes passed before I crawled out of the bed someone had put me in. Or did THEY put me here? Who are THEY? My head began to throb again. I sat down on the edge of the bed. I felt my clothes. It seemed like I was dressed in a jump suit, with snaps running up the front. I had on a pair of socks, but no shoes. What the hell is wrong with me and where am I? "JENNIFER" I shouted, waiting for some sort of response. Nothing! I didn't hear my voice. "I must be deaf. Oh, My GOD!"

I tried to get up once again, but felt too dizzy. Shaking my head didn't help, so I laid back down on the hard bed without any pillow. I felt cold and began to shake feverishly. My teeth chattered. I passed out.

I awoke again and felt like, maybe, I was normal. I sat up and swung my feet onto the floor and screamed, "Jennifer, where are you?" I still didn't hear my voice. I waited for a response, but none came, so I got up and moved slowly, holding my arms out in front of me until my fingers touched a wall. Possibly, a wall of rough cement, but not sure. I turned right and moved slowly, until my fingers touched another wall. I found the corner and traced along the other wall with my fingers, stopping at an indentation. It was a door, a steel door without a handle or knob. "JENNIFER" I shouted at the door. I pounded on the door and screamed, or I thought I had screamed. I know I had pounded because my hand hurt. I moved further along the wall until I came to another corner. It was all uneven cement. I moved further until I ran into the bed, a single bunk. I ran my fingers everywhere on the wall until I came to another wall. I continued running my fingers on this wall, until I found an opening. It was a small opening about six inches square. I stuck my arm into the hole and felt air flowing. I took some deep breaths before I screamed at the top of my lungs, "HELP! HELP!" I still couldn't hear my voice.

I located the bed, sat down and began to pray. I prayed like I had never prayed before. I waited for an instant reply from God. Nothing happened. I began to cry hysterically, or at least I thought I cried, but I didn't hear any sound. I became sleepy, lying down on the hard cot. My eyes shut without me closing them. I was asleep, I guess.

Chapter 45
A PRAYER IS ANSWERED

I awakened to a noise of metal against metal. "I can hear!" I whispered. Someone tried to open my door. Startled, I quickly flung my feet off the bed and walked toward the door. As I reached the door, it flew open, sending a bright beam of light into my room, blinding me. "I can see. I'm not blind." I whispered. I tried opening my eyes again, shading them with my left hand, leaving my right hand ready for defense, if needed.

A man's gruff voice rebounded off the walls into my brain telling me he spoke English, but with an accent. "Here is your breakfast." He handed me a small, tin tray with a tin bowl of cooked rice, without any spoon. He appeared to be an average-sized man.

"Where am I? Where is Jennifer? I want to talk to an attorney." The door slammed shut before I got the last word out of my mouth. I walked slowly back to my bed in the dark and sat down. I smelled the rice and ate some by dishing it out with my fingers. Realizing the rice was cold made things even worse. I ate it, but needed water.

I laid on my bed thinking, until the noise came again at the door. It seemed like hours had passed, but it was probably only an hour or so. I jumped up quickly, or as quickly as I could, without having had any water and a minimal amount of food. A man flung open the door. Only this time, he grabbed my left arm with a strong grip and led me out of my dungeon. My eyes tried to adjust to the glare of sunlight. We made it to the outside, the air being a whole lot better than it had been inside my cement room. I stumbled beside the man who walked at a fast pace. Sand and rock were everywhere. There were a few small buildings and other objects, like tents, scattered around. It looked like large mountains off in a distance, but the sun's glare blinded my vision. The temperature was cool.

We entered a building a couple of city blocks from where I had been held. I looked around to try and spot anything familiar. Nothing did, but I now believed I was in a foreign country, definitely not New Zealand.

Chapter 46
MEETING WITH THE ENEMY

Having been shoved down in a wooden chair about ten feet inside the entrance of a small building, I saw Arabic writing on the wall. At least, I thought it to be Arabic writing. I shook my head in disbelief. Was I ever in New Zealand with Jennifer? Was I captured by State Troopers in Illinois, or were they just disguised as Illinois State Patrolmen? The New Zealand part was a dream, a dream which never happened. So confused, I wanted to scream. "Jennifer" I whispered with my eyes closed. Before I opened them, another man, with darker skin than mine, led me briskly down the hall to another room. The door opened and then closed after we entered. In front of me sat four men behind a large wooden table, all dressed in some kind of military clothing. There were three men with machine guns, with one man standing on each side of the table and another one by the left wall.

"Mr. Sam Abbott, come in and have a seat. We need to talk to you," the oldest of the four said. He spoke very good English. He probably had received his education in a US College. After being slammed down hard by my escort, I sat there in my red jump suit, with no shoes on my feet.

"What is going on? Where am I? I want a pair of shoes." My eyes switched from one man to the other three, waiting for answers. They all stared back at me with half-smiles. They were all Arabs, I thought. The word, "terrorist," lay in my mouth, along with Taliban and Al-Queda.

"Mr. Abbott, you were kidnapped in Illinois by the Russians. Then, you were captured by us." They all laughed at me.

"Who are you? What did you do with my wife?"

"Shut up, Mr. Abbott. You speak when we ask you to speak."

"Did your government kill all of my employees and my wife?" I asked, with pain in my heart.

"Shut up, Mr. Abbott." The same man spoke again.

Another Arab man spoke, with a smile, "Your CIA killed all your employees and your wife and tried to kill you, but you were very lucky. The gas they used kills everyone but the smallest number of the population. You will, however, become sick and have tremendous headaches from your exposure. You will have nightmares, with sweats. They will come and go. Eventually, they will go away for good, but this will take weeks. You are very lucky to be alive."

"Why did the CIA kill my employees and my wife?" I trembled.

"Mr. Abbott, GREED is a very big word in your country and has gotten your government and most of its people in a great deal of trouble. Once your news media finds out members of the CIA did the killing, they will panic. The CIA acted on orders given by a prominent US Senator. Several of your largest drug companies' executives were involved, along with a large law firm in New York City. They already have been captured by your FBI for the deaths of all your employees, including your brother and your wife. Your country will fold up like an accordion. Your stock market will collapse within a week; your banks will fail within a month; and your companies will fold before year's end." He chuckled as if he couldn't wait to see the things he told me really happen.

I couldn't speak. I managed to get "water" out and was brought a cold glass of it. I gulped it down, not knowing what I was drinking, and asked for more, being very dehydrated. After the third glass of water, I spoke up. "Who's behind all this? Who's the main man?"

"A very popular US Senator from the State of Mississippi, Senator Sterling Shear, is your money man and the brains behind the whole plan. He is worth millions and was paid a billion from three of your top drug companies to collapse your company."

"My God, why didn't the drug companies just buy me out? Why kill all of them? My wife, Jennifer, didn't have to die. They knocked all her teeth out and cut off her fingers and toes and dumped her in a lake." I threw up the water I had just drunk.

The liquid from my stomach was quickly removed from the floor by one of the Arabic men outside the door, who was summoned by one of the four who sat at the table. "Mr. Abbott, your serum is very important to us. It is worth billions to us."

"How did you learn about the CIA being involved? They have such tight security and everything is classified."

"We have informants everywhere—the same as your government, or the same as Russia. The Russians can't keep their mouths shut when they've drunk too much vodka. The US can be bought. We, however, use a drug, a very intense truth serum, which gets us all the info we need. We are the only people with such a powerful truth serum. We knew about the priest in Chicago and every move you made since you left your compound in Georgia. So did the Russians. We knew about the tunnels under your compound before your CIA did. We were going to take over your compound, ourselves, but let your CIA guys do it, which left us out of the picture. We captured one of the CIA guys and he told us everything. The truth serum really does work." He chuckled and the others followed suit.

"When did you take me away from the Russians?"

"Ten miles down the road from where you were stopped. We saw the whole thing play out via a sophisticated satellite system only known to us."

"Who are you?"

"Taliban"

"What happened to Jo? Jo, the lady I was with in the Honda?" I wanted to use Cheryl's fictitious name. My throat felt parched, again.

"She is okay. She is not far from here. We will let her go as soon as we get the ransom for your serum." He gave me a wide grin, showing stained teeth from cigarettes, I guessed.

"What about my identification, credit card, driver's license, and my clothes?"

"We have all of it, but you won't need it. We will give you new clothes and shoes after we receive the money for your serum." Smiling, he showed his stained teeth, again.

"I want to see Jo."

"Not at this time, Mr. Abbott.

"Who's going to pay the ransom for me?"

"I don't know yet. We have several countries wanting you: Russia, China, the US, India, and even Iran is showing some interest."

"Where am I?"

"We will tell you when your ransom is paid." The four men rose and marched, single file, out of the room through a back door.

Chapter 47
FBI OFFICE – WASHINGTON D.C.

J im Kelly sat in his office staring out the window into the dark clouds, looking for answers to the directive he had been given by the President. He picked up the phone and called Jim Brewer's office. The phone rang three times before Brewer picked up on his restricted cell phone. His caller ID alerted him as to who was calling. "Brewer here, what do you need Jim?"

"Jim, I need to talk to you about what the President had to say today," Kelly said, tapping his fingers on his desk.

"You call it, Jim; name the place and the time and I will be there."

"We have a secure conference room over here. How about in two hours at my office."

"I'll be there." Brewer wanted to hang them all out to dry. Was it worth the risk of his kids not having the money to attend college? The risk of his wife, of after twenty five years, not being able to spend the money she was used to? The risk of being hung out to dry and, maybe, having trouble getting a job as a cop in a small city out in Wyoming?

Chapter 48

BREWER AND KELLY MEETING

Brewer arrived ten minutes early; Jim was waiting for him. They both wanted justice. They went into the secured room on Pennsylvania Ave. and closed the door. Knowing they had the meat cleaver in their hands, it was now up to them to use it and bring Washington DC to its knees. They were aware of the corruption which ran rampant in DC and filtered into the States, cities and all the way down to the small towns in America. It had to stop: NOW.

"Screw these bastards. They have to be tried and put away forever. We need to clean this filth up in Washington. This is only the beginning. I couldn't sleep knowing what I know and this SOB Shear runs off to some sandy beach with a billion dollars. He has the President in the palm of his hands, along with many other crooked political leaders," Kelly began. He stared at Brewer, hoping his response would be the same.

"It makes me sick to think my own men were involved in this. I just found out an hour ago that Shear and his rotten son and his buddies in the CIA have been involved for many years in a drug trafficking scheme with the cartels in Columbia. Jim, it is a billion dollar business run by Shear and they have been running it right under my nose. They're the same members of the CIA who attacked SAWWS Inc."

"I want to expose this to the media ASAP, Jim." Kelly spoke firmly.

"I'm with you 100%," Brewer replied. A flash of his family's needs traveled through his head like a hot air balloon.

"I believe we need to break this to the Washington Post immediately," Kelly said. "It's okay by me. What about Abbott? Where's Abbott and what happens to him?" Brewer asked.

"The Russians captured him in Illinois, along with the lady who supposedly killed Woody Saunders down in Georgia. We are trying to locate them as we speak," Kelly responded.

"Are you kidding me? Abbott's been running with Saunders' killer?" Brewer stood.

"The Russians wanted Abbott to give them SAWWS Inc.'s serum recipe. Abbott's been running with the Saunders killer since he left Georgia. We believe he picked her up along the way. We can't find any association between them prior to Abbott's disappearance. We have positive proof Saunders' car sat in the massage lady's driveway. The car had been removed by a tow truck, but his body lay in her house, which doesn't make any sense. Why not leave both car and body, or remove both? She might have killed him in self defense. Her customers have testified he had stalked her in the past."

"How did the Russians know of Abbott's whereabouts when they captured him in Illinois?"

"Informants, we think, but we aren't sure yet. It is also possible they used satellites to track him."

"How did you know the Russians captured Abbott and the lady who supposedly killed Saunders?"

"We used Russian informants."

"Woody Saunders' case is out of my responsibility, but I sure will try and help you find closure."

Kelly dialed Harold Reynolds, an old friend from college, at his office at the Washington Post. Kelly had always promised Reynolds a worthy topic, but never could due to security issues. Not this time. They had proof.

Reynolds walked into FBI headquarters within half an hour. Reynolds happened to be in the proximity, but dropped what he'd been working on and came directly to see his old friend.

Kelly's cell phone rang right after Reynolds sat down with them. "This is Jim Kelly." The pain on Kelly's face grew seconds after he spoke. Kelly set his phone down slowly, staring at the table top. The Taliban has Abbott and wants twenty billion for him in cash. China and Russia will match it, but the Taliban wants China and Russia out of the picture. Without the serum, Russia and China will collapse from two life-threatening disease epidemics. SAWWS Inc.'s serum would prevent the deaths from these two diseases."

"Wow!" Reynolds said, writing on his note pad.

"Can our government raise this kind of money?" Brewer asked, knowing the US never pays ransom.

"Don't print this in the Post, Harold."

"I won't print it. Just let me know what, where, and when on Abbott."

"I will, Harold."

Kelly and Brewer turned over all the information they had on SAWWS Inc. to Reynolds, to be printed by the Post. Reynolds promised not to publish anything without Brewer and Kelly reviewing it beforehand.

Chapter 49
BREAKING NEWS

The Washington Post broke the story, leaving out the ransom information, in the Thursday morning early edition. The President was informed about the story five minutes after he had sat down at his desk in the oval office; the time, 8:18 am. His press secretary, a guy in his late thirties named Wesley Roberts, spit out the words in a trembling voice, as he clutched the Washington Post tightly in his right hand. He waved the paper as he spoke. Roberts paused to catch his breath. He waited less than five seconds before the President, with eyes peering like an owl seeking its prey, tried to speak. His lips moved, but no sound came out of his mouth.

Finally, the President spoke. "Wha-what the hell happened? How did this get out to the damn media?" The President's face turned red; he jumped out of his chair, searching for an answer as to who had leaked this info.

"Sir, Mr. President." The President turned quickly and stared at his press secretary. "Kelly and Brewer informed Reynolds at the Post. They told him everything, naming names, including who were arrested. They indicated the investigation of many more political leaders, including you, Mr. President, will begin immediately." His voice trailed off on the last words, as his eyes fell to the floor.

The President stared at Roberts with rage building throughout his whole body. "Kelly and Brewer are finished. Those SOBs shouldn't have done this. WHY? I told them this could not be leaked to the damn press." Thoughts of past sexual encounters buzzed through his head one last time. The President moved slowly and fell into his chair. He now looked pale, turning from red-faced to ashen-faced. "I don't feel good. That bastard Shear!" These were to be the last words spoken by the President. The President clutched his chest and died instantly in the same chair where, previously, Brandi had serviced him on numerous occasions. The President never read a word of the Post article.

Wesley Roberts panicked and screamed, "HELP! HELP!" Within seconds, three members of the President's secret service, who were positioned outside the oval office, arrived on the scene. McMullen, the senior agent, asked, "What's the matter with the President?"

"He just collapsed. He clutched his chest. Oh, My God!" Roberts said, placing his hand over his mouth. Roberts stood paralyzed as he watched the secret service men tend to the President.

Agent Jenkins administered CPR immediately, with no response. Olson, the third secret service agent, called dispatch to have the President rushed to Walter Reed Hospital.

Within three minutes from the time Olson had made his call, two men with a gurney barged through the door. They quickly loaded the President on the gurney and raced him to the helicopter sitting on the pad behind the White House.

At 9:10 am, less than an hour after Wesley Roberts had entered the oval office to inform the President of the Washington Post article, the President was pronounced dead.

They withheld the news of the death of the President until after the President's wife and family had been notified. An emergency meeting was held at 10:00 that same morning with the Vice President, the speaker of the house, and the majority leaders of both the Senate and the House. Everyone in the meeting feared the worst. They weren't worried about the country, the stock market, the bank failures—only for themselves. They were all guilty and were all afraid the FBI or the CIA would drag them down the toilet. They knew they could be tried and prosecuted for their shenanigans and the corruption they had gotten away with for so many years. Everyone in the room was categorized as a multimillionaire. Most of their assets sat in foreign banks so they could avoid paying taxes. Sad, but true.

Chapter 50

THE STOCK MARKET

The stock market opened at 9:30 am Thursday with a drop in the DOW of 1000 points. When the news broke later in the day of the President's death, the market tumbled another 2000 points. The market closed immediately to avoid a crash. The political leaders, both Republicans and Democrats, in Washington were very nervous; especially, the ones who had been bought off by Senator Shear, which also included the lobbyists who prey on Washington's steps.

The television and radio media beat the story to death. European markets nose dived quickly on the news of Shear's plans to destroy SAWWS Inc. They closed before learning of the President's death.

Opening bell Friday in Europe brought total chaos and an extraordinarily large sell off. Unemployment in Europe was much higher than in the States at the time. The news of the US problems with government officials and the drastic drop in the market brought fear to banks and businesses throughout Europe. China waited in the distance to take over. They wouldn't even have to fire one rocket or spend one shell. The collapse of the free world appeared to be near, with the Chinese holding large bank notes from all the free world countries. GREED WAS DESTROYING THE FREE WORLD QUICKLY AND ITS PEOPLE LET IT HAPPEN.

The news spread rapidly and brought fear, hate, and revenge from every employee, non-employee and business owner throughout every country on the globe.

Where does it stop? It stops with Jim Kelly and Jim Brewer blowing the lid off the large cesspool of slime. They were the only ones with the guts to say, "Enough is enough." They made Washington's corrupt political leaders confess to their corruption, which took the USA down Devastation Road.

Chapter 51
HOLLOWAY'S RESPONSE

D avid Holloway, listed as the wealthiest person on earth, made all his money honestly. He paid an enormous sum of taxes every year. He never put a dime in foreign banks. Holloway lived in a moderate home, valued at less than $400,000. He made Warren Buffet look middle class. Because of his charitable causes worldwide and his financial contribution in starting up SAWWS Inc., Mr. Holloway was named the most popular person on earth.

Holloway had spoken up many times about the political system in Washington and had been asked many times to seek public office to try to rectify the corruption.

David Holloway had appeared often on television news shows to speak about our country's electoral system, government waste, federal spending, the fighting in wars we never win, immigration, the prison system, the educational system, bringing jobs back to USA, Medicare, obesity, social security, and foreign aide. Holloway never cared if he stepped on some political leader's toes, whether it was a senator, congressman, or even the President of the US. He wanted the public to be aware of what transpired in Washington. David Holloway was registered as an Independent voter.

David Holloway called Jim Kelly's office three hours after the Post made the story public. His personal secretary, Miss Nancy Crane, had received a telephone call at 4:28a.m. Pacific Time informing her of the Post article. The call came from an employee of one of Holloway's companies in the east. She notified Holloway by cell phone at 5:00 a.m. Pacific Time. With the three hour time difference between Washington DC and Seattle, Washington, Holloway waited till Jim Kelly had had his coffee and time to digest the events of his early morning. He instructed his secretary, Nancy, to call the pilots and crew of his private jet.

Kelly and Holloway were on a first-name basis. They had met three years ago on an FBI investigation of one of Holloway's companies. It was concerning a patent on some high tech digital camera, which had been confiscated by some outside source through one of Holloway's employees. It took a year before they nailed the man who was involved. The FBI had two agents, one female and the other male, inside Holloway's company for almost a year. Holloway and Kelly had conversed many times, both in person and on the phone, about the corruption in Washington.

"Good Morning, David," Kelly responded, after his secretary had patched the call from Holloway over to Kelly's phone.

"It is a great morning, Jim. I can't tell you how much respect I have for you and Jim Brewer to get the Post to open up about the people responsible for the deaths of the employees of SAWWS Inc."

"David, I couldn't sleep letting these bastards in Washington off the hook another day. Justice has to be done and screw the political correctness."

"I couldn't agree more, Jim." Holloway knew what he wanted to say and never had been lost for words ever since he'd been on a debate team in college when he fumbled around on a subject he had not been versed on. "Jim, with all the things happening in this nation in the last few hours and now with the President's death, I believe this country will sink to a level none of us has ever fathomed."

"You're absolutely correct, David. I was actually going to call you to have you come to Washington and meet with Brewer and me. We need a leader in this nation, immediately. We have enough on the Vice President to bury him in federal prison, not to mention the Speaker of the House, the Secretary of State, Secretary of Defense, and many more political leaders here in Washington. Republican or Democrat, they are all as guilty as Castro."

"Jim, I will be out of here in four and a half hours. Do you have a personal connection with the military?"

"Yes, David. I am very good friends with General Brandon Mathews of the Army and also General Scott Thomas of the Air Force."

"What about our Navy, Coast Guard and Marines? We need all military personnel on our side, Jim."

"I'll get them on the phone."

"Great, Jim, have them meet us in five hours, along with Jim Brewer."

"I'll pick you up at Reagan upon your arrival. Brewer will be with me so we can have a briefing before meeting with the Generals."

"Thanks, Jim."

Holloway dialed another number immediately after hanging up with Kelly. He called Richard Morehouse, an expert in foreign relations. Richard, a Yale graduate, had more than thirty years experience in foreign affairs and, most recently, served as the American Ambassador to China for one, eight-year administration. Prior to that, he had been the American Ambassador to Saudi Arabia for another eight-year administration. He performed these duties impeccably. Richard, with his popularity at high levels, had been summoned by the Republican Party to run for President on two different occasions. He refused both times.

"Good morning, David. I guess it is a good morning."

"Good morning, Richard." David eyeballed his digital clock sitting on his desk in his home outside Seattle. "This country is heading in a downward spiral and it needs to change course without delay."

"Where do you want to meet?" Richard knew how David operated.

"Washington DC, today, at 3:00, at FBI headquarters on Pennsylvania Ave."

"I will be there, David." Richard lived in Dallas, Texas with his wife, Maria.

On the second ring, Stanley Armstrong answered in a deep baritone voice, "Good morning, David." Armstrong, with an MBA in finance from Harvard, was the CEO of the largest banking system in the USA. They were solvent and Stanley aimed to keep it that way. Stanley resided in Oakbrook, Illinois, outside of Chicago. Holloway had used Armstrong's banks for many years.

"Stanley, I need you in Washington at FBI Headquarters on Pennsylvania Ave at 3:00 today." Stanley also knew how David operated when time was of the essence.

"See you at 3:00, David." Stanley thumbed through his calendar to see what had to be canceled.

The next call went to Andrew Huggins. Huggins, a 220 pound, broad shouldered, black, retired Marine Colonel, lived in Atlanta, Georgia. Since his retirement from the Marine Corps four years ago, Huggins had headed up a private security company. This security company was unheard of to the media and the American public since it was only used in special assignments. His employees consisted of former Navy Seals, Army Delta and Marine Special Forces. They were highly trained in protecting, securing, monitoring, and maintaining order, regardless of the circumstance or location.

"Good morning, David. I expected to hear from you this morning."

"Andrew, we need to meet in DC, at FBI Headquarters, today, at 1500 hours.

"I'll be there, Sir." Huggins hoped his team would be needed. Not for the money, but for the democracy of the nation and to bring this nation back to where it once was.

The clock ticked by, lapsing 52 minutes since Nancy had called her boss. Holloway, still in his bathrobe and bedroom slippers, hadn't had breakfast yet. The Holloways didn't have any maid service. His wife, Marilyn, had gone to her niece's in Minneapolis, where her niece was about to give birth to a boy. He needed to call Nancy to inform her about his departure time and the duration of time he would be spending in Washington. He could grab some breakfast on his private jet.

The last call made before Holloway turned the shower on was to John Manchester, a former Rhodes Scholar, with a PhD in Physiology, a PhD in terminal illnesses, and presently the head of the School of Medicine at Johns Hopkins University.

"Good morning, Mr. Holloway." Manchester was born in England and his English mannerisms have never left him.

"John, I need to have your ideas in Washington DC, at FBI headquarters, at 3:00 today."

"Certainly, Mr. Holloway, I will be there. Is there anything in particular you want so I can be more prepared?"

"I can't really explain it now, John, but let's just say your expertise will be greatly appreciated. You could speak for hours on medical subjects, no teleprompter needed."

"Mr. Holloway, I will be there. It is an honor to have you call me with such an enormous invitation."

"Thank you, John."

Holloway headed for the showers.

Chapter 52

FBI HEADQUARTERS—
WASHINGTON DC

David Holloway stood behind the lectern with no notes. "Gentlemen, I want to thank all of you for being here on such short notice. You all have been briefed on the disaster this country is in. I need everyone's expertise today on how we should handle, evaluate, judge, elect, eliminate and replace our government structure. I have some ideas I want to pass on to you this morning. We have enough evidence on just about every Senator and Representative to put them behind bars. The President's cabinet will also be asked to resign, but all will be monitored until final investigative results are in. If they are found guilty, or not guilty, they will be either prosecuted or removed from office. We have enough information on the Vice President to put him away for life. I suggest we eliminate all of them from their offices by 5:00 tomorrow. A clean slate is our only answer." All heads nodded simultaneously.

"Four groups will be formed among all in attendance here today to discuss the top priorities needed to rectify the situations we are facing. I have drawn up a list of these and have made copies for all of you. These priorities, I believe, need to be put into law immediately. Believe me, we have other issues, but these need to be handled pronto. If any of you gentlemen have any other concerns, please let me know and we will discuss them here today." Holloway paused to drink a half glass of water.

"Russia's government is sick about the capture of Sam Abbott and having lost him to the Taliban. Russia has an epidemic and tens of thousands are dying. It is a virus which SAWWS Inc.'s serum can eliminate. Russia's economy is almost in total collapse because of the outbreak of this deadly virus.

"Japan is trying to dig out from another tsunami, which has paralyzed the entire country. They have a serious typhoid outbreak. They are on the verge of a deep depression.

"Europe stood in total shambles before the SAWWS Inc. murders. They are now in a depression, with banks closing and the rich stealing from the poor. Their medical program is broke and the sick are not being cared for. The death rate per day in Europe is much higher than during World War II and is expected to double in the next year. The news in the USA will bring Europe to its knees, immediately.

"The Muslims thought they could control the world with oil, their only revenue producer; but with the world's debacle, oil prices are slashed and output is at a standstill. Iran, Iraq, Libya, and Saudi Arabia, the big four oil producing nations in the world, will become skeletons in the sand. Maybe not a bad thing, but the world's balance sheet jumps when oil goes up or down." David cleared his throat, swallowed some water and continued.

"China, however, is holding billions of dollars in bank notes from many countries throughout the world. The USA is the largest. They can call those bank notes whenever they wish, giving them world control.

China has the greatest population of any country in the world and the largest military and space program. It is the highest revenue producing nation, the largest export nation and the most high-tech nation, only because the USA gave them the tools and education to become number one. With the SAWWS Inc. serum, they can control not only their population, but also the world's population.

"This collapse started to happen back in the 70's when the USA began sending a large portion of its manufacturing to China and then shipped it back to the States to be consumed by the greedy public. This grew and grew and within two decades, the USA was manufacturing hardly any furniture, clothing, shoes, small appliances, etc. The US companies moved their manufacturing to China, Vietnam, Indonesia, and other Asian countries, where they could get cheap labor. They then charged almost the same for the product. This made the stockowners very happy. Nobody seemed to care—everybody was making money, except the US worker, who had lost his job to an Asian country. He, or she, eventually moved on to the service field, making less money but spending more—the American way.

"Before the turn of the 21st century, our imports more than doubled over our exports. We still have Boeing, Caterpillar, automobiles, cigarettes, 3M, meat, wheat, corn, cotton, etc., to export. Many of our American-made automobile parts are made in Mexico and sent back to our assembly lines in the US. Greedy auto manufacturers wanted more profit so did away with thousands of jobs here in the States.

"The US Government has been sending millions of dollars abroad in aid every year. Yet, we have over half of our working population out of work, living in poverty, collecting welfare, and not paying any taxes. The reason, as I see it, is there is no one in Washington lobbying for them to help them find jobs. If US political leaders don't get a kickback, then forget about them helping anyone. This is why Senators and Congressmen spend millions to get elected. They don't want the job to help the working consumer—they want the position to make millions for themselves from large corporations, countries we send aid to, government projects being built or remodeled, such as roads and bridges, and let's not forget all the pork belly projects." Holloway drank some water and shifted his weight before he began again.

"Saudi Arabia is one of the richest countries in the world. The main reason is the greedy, free world using billions of barrels of Saudi oil to move them from place to place. US oil companies have sucked up billions, not to mention the hungry stockowners of these oil companies, by buying Saudi, Iraqi, Iranian and Libyan oil and selling it to the people of the US and other countries.

"Saudi Arabia has become the financial support base for Al Queda, Taliban, and Hamas. Billions of Saudi money is laundered through Wazrirstan, Afghanistan, a city on the border of Afghanistan and Pakistan. In 2002, the Saudi government bragged about the royal family and Saudi kingdom spending billions of dollars to spread Islam to every corner of the earth. It has succeeded and is growing rapidly.

"Saudi funds were used to build over 1500 Mosques, 202 colleges, and 201 Islamic centers in the US. These centers can be found in: Los Angeles and San Francisco, CA; Chicago; New York; Washington DC; Tucson, Arizona; Raleigh, North Carolina; and Toledo, Ohio.

"Europe has over 6000 Mosques spread throughout the continent. The US, where freedom of religion is protected by our constitution, has over 2000 Mosques and growing.

"Saudi's billions own many shares in American businesses, controlling a large percentage of the New York Stock Exchange. The State of Tennessee has three large Islamic complexes located in Memphis, Antioch, and Murphysboro. Brooklyn, New York just opened a large Mosque. Atlanta, Georgia opened a 10-million dollar mosque in 2008. Then, there is Roxbury, Massachusetts, who welcomed a 60-million dollar Islamic center.

"The Saudis have spent huge sums on donations to major universities in the US since 9/11. Over 80,000 Saudis are being educated in these same universities, leaving thousands of young Americans having to seek out smaller universities. Our government doesn't disclose the true extent of the Saudi financial input into our political machine, educational and social services in America. Thirty years prior to 9/11 the words Islamic, Mosques, and Taliban were rarely mentioned, if at all.

"Inside the US borders, you can find over 35 million Islamic people living in the land of opportunity. Many Islamic people in this country tell our local leaders their wants and needs in reference to education, religion, and State and local regulations." David looked carefully at his audience and said, "I will get off my band wagon." He moved away from the lectern.

Before he sat down, he suggested, "How about taking 90 minutes to discuss these items I spoke of earlier and then we will break for lunch."

After a catered lunch paid for by David Holloway, he called the meeting to order in the same room Brewer and Kelly had talked before deciding to blow the lid off the corruption in the political nightmare in Washington. Everyone David Holloway had called came with concern, but ready to help in any way they could to get the USA back to normalcy.

"The items I laid out for this meeting have been discussed among yourselves in various groups. I suggest, with the current state of world affairs, we immediately secure our borders. Can this be done this week, if we start bringing all our troops home?" All military generals agreed, without hesitation.

General Mathews spoke up. "We can also call up all our National Guard personnel to help secure our borders."

"This may be asking too much, but I would like to see every person entering our country fingerprinted and all pertinent information recorded, enabling us to track each person. Individuals would be allowed to stay only one week and must report, while they are on our soil, his or her whereabouts everyday to our military intelligence," Holloway said. All agreed.

"I want to bring all troops home, immediately, to be used to protect, control and maintain peace through these turbulent times. We definitely will be putting out fires from radical groups throughout the country. Our National Guard would probably come into play here, as well," Holloway continued. Again, everyone agreed.

"I would like an immediate canvassing of this entire country by our military once all troops are back on our soil to eliminate all illegal immigrants, who are squatting on our soil. I think every square inch should be covered, starting from our northern borders to our southern borders. All illegal immigrants will be escorted across the border or shipped back to their country." Everyone agreed.

"I think we need to change our Constitution's election procedures in order to get this country back where we, the people, have control of where the money goes. We need to elect government people to replace these Senators and Representative who have stolen, defrauded, embezzled and cheated the American public out of billions of dollars. I suggest we have a one party system, 'FOR THE PEOPLE.' An election would be held in each State and two people would represent each State, regardless of population. I suggest a four-year term, with a salary of $50,000 per member, per year. I would rather see former successful business executives serving our country, than some rich lawyers. No fringe benefits—period." Everyone applauded David's last statement.

"Since we have a catastrophe in our health care system in this country, we need to correct it ASAP. All recipients of any government health care program should be drug screened, immediately. All food stamp recipients should be drug screened, immediately. All food stamps are to be used only by individuals assigned and should not be able to be sold. No illegal immigrant will be entitled to any government assistance, whether education, medical or food." Everyone agreed.

"Elimination of all foreign aid until this country is debt free."
All nodded.

"Pay off our debt to all foreign countries ASAP, especially China.

"I would like to see a simple, flat income tax for every individual of no more than 7%. No tax deductions." All agreed.

"Eliminate all lobbyists in Washington." Everyone applauded.

"Gentlemen, we have a tremendous undertaking in front of us. We will have the ACLU, and other activist groups, protesting. I suggest we politely ask them to stop or they will be arrested by our military." Everyone nodded.

"One final, serious problem you are all aware of." David hesitated for a few seconds before speaking again. "Sam Abbott has been captured by the Taliban and is being held for ransom. China and Russia have offered a large sum of money for Sam. I don't want the US to pay any ransom. I want our country to get Abbott and bring him back alive. I have asked Andrew Huggins to be here today. With the help of our military's top soldiers and Andrew's men, we need to bring Abbott home. We need Sam Abbott back to work making the serum needed to not only protect the American people, but also our allies."

Jim Brewer spoke next. "Our military intelligence has pinpointed the position where the Taliban group is holding Sam Abbott. This operation, PINPOINT, will go into effect approximately 24 hours from now. I want General Mathews to report on our plan."

General Mathews stood 6 foot 2 inches, with broad shoulders and grey temples. "We will deploy a group of soldiers and Huggins' men outside of Waziristan, Afghanistan. They are holding Sam Abbott up near the mountain region outside of Waziristan. It won't be too much longer before they will use a potent truth serum on Abbott." Mathews stared down at the podium as if he were asking for God's help.

Mathews cleared his throat and began again. "The Taliban doesn't want the serum. They want the money the serum is worth, from whoever will pay them the most money. I don't want any of the hostage takers left alive. We will use paratroopers from the 82nd Airborne Division and Huggins' men. We are also going to drop in six humvees south of the border, approximately 50 miles from where Abbott is being held. The paratroopers will have to hoof it out to the humvees over rugged, mountain terrain. We expect heavy resistance from the Taliban after we grab Abbott. The mountain region has hundreds of Taliban hiding in the area. General Thomas, of the Air Force, has assured me his fighter planes will give us all the air support we need. The humvees will carry the men out and take them to a NATO airfield in Pakistan. From there, Sam Abbott will be transferred home on a military aircraft to Reagan International. The military plane will be escorted by six fighter jets at all times, until the plane lands here in DC. The Navy and Air Force will be involved in the escort."

Holloway spoke again. "I will address the public on TV and radio this evening at 10:00 EST. I am hopeful the majority of the people will be in favor. Military control may scare many people, but we have no choice in order to get this country back to where it needs to be. I want to thank everyone, again, for attending today. We will meet again tomorrow morning at 0800 right here. I would like each of you to be prepared to share your thoughts on what I have proposed today."

Chapter 53
OPERATION PINPOINT

Thirty-four courageous men, including retired Colonel Andrew Huggins, arrived at Ramstein Air Force base, Germany, at 0400 hours, the following morning. Eighteen of these men came from Huggins' operation, all paratroopers and highly trained in covert operations, with more than 200 jumps per man. Twelve more paratroopers with a minimum of 100 jumps each reported from the 82nd Airborne Division. The remaining four men, Huggins, two pilots and loadmaster, are to remain on board. Huggins will monitor the operation and report, via high security cell phone, to Tony Spellini, a twenty-year, retired Senior Master Sergeant, the leader of the mission. All were briefed on the mission to recover Sam Abbott from the compound where he was being held captive.

Members of the 82nd Airborne Division, Huggins' men, two pilots and the loadmaster, left on a C-130J, which has the capacity to carry up to 42,000 pounds, maximum payload and a maximum cruising altitude of 34,000 feet at speeds in excess of 400 mph. The C-130J can fly 2000 miles without refueling. Two C-130 Hercules cargo carriers will take six hummers and drop them in Pakistan by parachutes. These hummers are 6 feet high, 7 feet wide and 15 feet long. They weigh 5200 lbs., with a payload of 2500 lbs. They come with diesel engines, power steering, and one, 25 gallon fuel tank, with a range of 300 miles per tank. The driver can lower the air pressure in the tires while sitting behind the wheel to give the vehicle a smoother ride, and also provide a better grip on rough terrain. These vehicles cost the government in the neighborhood of $65,000 each. Hummer, or humvee, is an acronym for: high mobility multi purpose wheeled vehicle.

All of the paratroopers on this mission received their training at Fort Benning, Georgia. The vigorous training took three weeks. The first week, ground week, is dedicated to learning how to pack their chutes; the do's and don'ts in order to stay alive, including high physical exercise; and included instructions on how to land, making sure knees and feet are together, to prevent injury. They also learned how to roll after hitting the ground. Many wannabes drop out the first week due to the stringent exercise program. The second week is tower week. They jump from a 34-foot tower followed by a jump from a 250-foot tower. The drop out rate triples the second week. No person is asked to be a paratrooper; it is strictly a volunteer program. The third week is jump week; they jump from a plane. The drop out rate drastically climbs the third week. All paratroopers in training are between the ages of 18 and 36.

At 0100 hours the next morning, a C-130J flew over the target zone. The troop door opened, with thirty armed men lined up ready to jump. Each man carried a 35 pound MT1X parachute, an M-4 Glock 19, knife, tourniquet, triangle bandage, dressings, spare parts, tool kit, batteries, flashlight, pistol belt and night vision glasses. Tony Spellini, the former Air Force Delta member, led the ground troops. Their mission was to take over, maintain and kill any enemy after Abbott's safe removal from the compound. Spellini, the first man out, landed in a grove of trees. After freeing himself from his parachute, he fell ten feet to the hard rock service below. Spellini walked hurriedly toward an open field. After scoping out the landing area for the troops, he dialed his boss, Huggins. "Huggy Bear, Trooper One" He waited; seconds later a transmission came back.

"Trooper One, Huggy Bear, here. We have position. The remaining troops will jump."

"Huggy Bear, Trooper One. The cloud covers up to 18,000 feet with wind speed steady at 11 mph. Proceed."

The night air was cold, -30 below F at 27,000 feet. It was heavily overcast, pitch black. The troops were going to do a HAHO jump, or high altitude high chute opening, so the Taliban would be unable to hear the plane. Huggins' men descended first, followed by the 82nd Airborne troops. The C-130J circled the area three times over the DZ, or drop zone; first to drop Spellini, then Huggins' men, then the 82nd Airborne Division. The wind remained steady at 11 mph. The coordinates for the drop, with the wind direction, would put the troops right on the DZ.

Each paratrooper wore a Patagonia undergarment to keep his body temperature warm from chilling temperatures, along with thorlo socks to keep his feet warm. A pair of night vision goggles mounted on his helmet equipped with a built-in GPS uses a tunnel vision so he can see where he is going.

Prior to jumping, each man took in 100% oxygen for 40 minutes in order to eliminate all nitrogen from the bloodstream. This prevents the bends in high altitude. In addition, each paratrooper will inhale 100% oxygen on his descent, which will prevent him from passing out. Hypoxia is a decompression sickness no paratrooper wants to have happen.

They proceeded to jump and hoped to have the compound where Abbott was being held secured and surrounded within 26 minutes from the time the last man hit the ground.

Chapter 54
ON THE GROUND

The troops all landed safely on the two-acre surface, just 1000 yards from Abbott. Each man had his itinerary melted in his brain. The thirty men scattered, as mapped out in Operation Pinpoint, and within ten minutes had the ten-acre compound surrounded and were closing in.

I sat in my tomb, on my bed, not knowing the time of day, waiting for my next meal. Not really hungry, just wanted something to do. Rice and water everyday, three times a day, until I die, seemed beyond reach. I hadn't uttered a sound to my enemy as to the elements of my serums. My stomach was drum tight from this daily diet. No bowel movement since Chicago. I had run out of prayers. I had thought of Cheryl many times, but had now blocked her out, due to my upcoming death and my loss of Jennifer and all my employees who tried so hard to help people live. I had asked God many times: Why me? Why my company? Why

Jennifer? Why my people? NO ANSWER! WHY? My hopes were now shattered. The truth serum they told me about may be my last resort. The serum would give them the information. What good am I to them? My time is fatal. No more time.

A few minutes passed when I heard gunfire. It sounded like it occurred outside my door. I waited several minutes then the locks on my door were shot off. Maybe the Russians have found me. I didn't hear any voices. Seconds passed and the door flew open. It was as dark as black ink. I couldn't see anything. "Abbott let's go. We're with the US Army and are here to take you back."

I sat dead still. My heart had stopped, I thought. I stayed frozen to the bed. Seconds later, two men lifted me off the bed. I couldn't see. They ran out the door carrying me. We were in a dead run. My arms were paralyzed from the grip these men had on me. My feet dragged on the ground, tearing my socks off. My feet burned from the stones and rocks on the ground. I still couldn't see where I was going. I heard a loud noise in the distance. "GUNFIRE! GET DOWN," someone ahead of us yelled. We hit the dirt. The gunfire became rapid and nonstop for several minutes.

The men from Huggins' group and the 82nd fired rapidly at the opposition. Wearing night vision goggles, they could see who they were shooting at. The enemy couldn't see their targets. Who was the enemy?

"Russian troops," Spellini shouted. "Kill them! They want Abbott. What the hell?" Spellini had taken a bullet in the shoulder. Rapid fire began, flashing light in the cool, midnight air.

I thought of Cheryl and wondered if they knew about her; or if they did, were they going to try and rescue her. "What about Cheryl?" I asked the soldier beside me. He never answered me. I shook his arm, wanting an answer, still not sure who had me lying in the brush without any socks on my bloody feet. I couldn't see anything. The man on my right had moved forward and fired his weapon from a prone position. The voices sounded like Americans, but so did the ones who had captured Cheryl and me in Illinois. I started to pray, when a bullet struck a rock in front of me, sending chips of rock into my face. I didn't have a helmet.

The gunfire ceased and the still, night air became dead quiet—dead as in a cemetery. The soldier, who helped carry me to this spot, spoke to me. "Where the hell are your shoes?"

"They took my shoes. I had socks on, but lost them on the way out here."

"Medic! Medic!"

Ten minutes later, or what seemed like ten minutes, a medic arrived on the scene. The medic reached into his bag of supplies and cleaned, medicated and wrapped my feet in bandages in a matter of a few minutes. Not a word had been spoken, until I asked about Cheryl.

"Sergeant Mosher has her. I gave her a tranquilizer to keep her calm. She doesn't know what is going on. We'll get both of you out of here safely within 24 hours. We have to go up that mountain ahead of us, then down the other side, where six Hummers are waiting for us. From there, we will go to a NATO airfield in Pakistan fifty miles and take a C-130 Hercules to Ramstein Air Force Base in Germany. I'll give you a tranquilizer, too, so the trip will be much easier for you, as well as for the two guys responsible for getting you on that C-130."

I said to the medic, "I can't see. I don't even know where the mountain is. Where in Pakistan are we? Who are you and what kind of drug are you going to stick in my arm?"

"My name is Sergeant Joe Arnold and I'm with the 82nd Air Borne Division. You're in good hands, Mr. Abbott," the medic said, as he spoke in my ear.

"Who captured me?"

"The Taliban and the Russians wanted you. Those were the Russians we just removed from the scene. You're the most wanted man in the world, but nobody's going to touch you now—nobody."

Sergeant Arnold stuck the needle in my right arm before I knew what was happening. Within a few seconds, my anxiety slithered out of my body.

Spellini was grazed and patched up quickly by Arnold, and now Spellini spat out the orders. "Keep your eyes focused. We still may have enemy in these hills ahead. We'll have air support from the Air Force on the other side of the mountain. When you hear the planes, don't stop, keep moving. Forward, march! Double time!" I felt dazed from the tranquilizer shot. I hadn't seen Cheryl. I realized two men were carrying me.

Spellini dialed Huggins after the command and gave him the coordinates of the troops.

The air strikes lasted for one hour. Paratroopers ran up the mountain, while their two guests were carried. On the way down the mountainside, Taliban soldiers lay scattered everywhere. The paratroopers raced down the other side, never stopping

Six Hummers were waiting at the base of the mountain. Six keys were in six different soldiers' pockets, the designated drivers for the operation.

Everyone climbed aboard the Hummers within minutes. Cheryl and I were handed up to the soldiers who were already on board. All six diesels started and they were off across the desert, with no lights on, moving over fifty miles per hour, using GPS all the way to the NATO airstrip.

I looked up at a large, black man and couldn't speak. I felt faint. Blurry came, then black appeared, and I fell sleep. I woke up later and found the large, black man sitting beside me, grinning. "You ready for some breakfast?"

After eating and finding out all the details of Senator Shear, his son, Travis, and all the other political leaders, my stomach was in knots. I didn't know if it was from eating too fast, eating American food or the whole, sudden discovery of what had transpired at SAWWS, Inc. They called David Holloway and informed him we were airborne on the C-130 Hercules.

"Hi, David! I know you probably had something to do with the rescue operation."

"I'm so glad you're safe and now heading to Germany. I'm so sorry about Jennifer, your brother, and all your employees. We need you back here, Sam."

"Thank you, David. They gave me a tranquilizer so when I come out of it, I might be different."

"Have a safe flight, Sam."

"Thanks, again, David."

Where's Cheryl? I looked around and saw nothing but sleeping soldiers. I tried to get up, but couldn't move. The tranquilizer was still working. Seconds later, Sergeant Arnold, the medic, knelt beside me. I didn't recognize him until he told me his name. Though, I did recall the southern accent as soon as he spoke. "How are you doing, Mr. Abbott? I'm Sergeant Arnold."

"I'm okay, I guess. Where is Cheryl? How is she doing? How much longer until I can function on my own? I can't even walk."

"You will be fine. We need to keep you sedated until after you are checked out at Ramstein Air Base by medical doctors. Once they give the okay, you will be flown by military plane back to Washington DC. As for Cheryl, she is resting, and is still heavily sedated for safety reasons. You both have been through a traumatic experience and will be guarded for several days until you both adjust to freedom. Cheryl will also be thoroughly examined at the medical facilities at Ramstein."

"Thanks, sergeant. How much longer before we land?"

"Two hours and 28 minutes," Arnold said after looking at his watch. He checked my heart and left. I closed my eyes, but kept opening them to make sure I was still on the plane and not in a black tomb. I finally went to sleep, I think.

Chapter 55

RAMSTEIN
AIR FORCE BASE

After two days of an intensive physical by several military doctors, they allowed me to visit Cheryl. I had lost twenty-five pounds since the day Jennifer and I were to depart for New Zealand, rice and water not being the kind of diet my body could handle. My feet were healing, thanks to Sergeant Arnold. They sent me to a military barber to have my hair washed and cut. They may have been checking for lice, bugs, or some other sand-living creatures.

Cheryl received the same type of physical. She had lost ten pounds, but still looked great, as we met in a small room in the military hospital. The room was painted in a light tan color, with a light beige carpet. A small sofa sat against the far wall, with a small table and four chairs in the center and some nature pictures hanging on all four walls. I had arrived first, but never sat down. I tried to piece everything together. The door opened and Cheryl walked in. Her partial smile told me she was holding tons of stress.

We walked hurriedly towards one another until we embraced. We held each other until the tears flowed from our eyes and sounds of crying filled the room. We squeezed each other tightly, trying to rid the anguish, fear, and emotion from our bodies and minds. Cheryl shook, sniffling, with tears forming streams down both cheeks. I finally spit out, "Did they hurt you? They didn't molest you, did they?" Knowing the Taliban treated their women like animals do in the wild.

Her eyes slowly shut and she nodded once. Her sniffling turned from light crying to a hysterical outburst. She tightened her grip on my shoulders, perhaps looking for warmth, protection, love, or, possibly, respect from the horrible days she had spent in captivity.

We sat down on the leather sofa; both of us stared at the wall facing us. "We are safe, now. Once we get back to the States, I will do everything I can to help you, either financially or emotionally." I kissed her on the cheek and tasted her salty tears. She hugged me and kissed me softly several times.

"Thank you, Sam. I haven't enough money to pay for a good lawyer. I only have enough scraped together to put down on a new car. Since those people kidnapped us, I just wanted to die and make everything go away. When our military rescued me, the thoughts of going back to the States and being tried for murder and sentenced to prison terrified me. I'm not sure I can handle it."

"I won't let you go to prison. I will get the best attorneys in America. You're innocent." I spoke, without having any money. My dry mouth hung open with those thoughts hanging on the edge of my lips, but said nothing. I didn't know where my money was. Her magic fingers worked on my frozen neck.

They gave us an hour. The time passed quickly. More thoughts of our future than words evaporated our time. I want to sell my company to somebody, probably a large drug company. I haven't the energy or the desire to run it anymore. I couldn't; and, no, I don't want to.

We hugged each other, again, before two female military personnel escorted Cheryl out and away from my reaching arms. "Stay strong," I managed to say before the door closed, leaving me alone. Less than a minute later, two military men escorted me back to my quarters.

Epilogue

S am Abbott spent several weeks in Washington DC going through debriefings and locating a legitimate drug company to purchase SAWWS Inc. The money in Abbott's checking and saving accounts, along with Jennifer's money from her checking and saving accounts, was recovered. The media was never informed of Abbott's whereabouts.

After an FBI investigation, Cheryl was acquitted of all charges. She spent several weeks at Georgetown University with various psychologists to help her cope with the trauma she had gone through. Again, her location was never shared with the media.

Cheryl and Sam eventually married and had three children. They live in protective custody and will do so for the remainder of their lives; their whereabouts, unknown.

Sterling Shear, the former US Senator from Mississippi, was sentenced to 699 years in a federal prison in solitary confinement. DEATH WOULD HAVE BEEN TOO EASY. His son and the other CIA agents involved in the death and destruction of SAWWS Inc. were sentenced to 499 years each, to be served in a different federal prison.

The former congressmen and senators were all sentenced to prison, with a maximum of 199 years and a minimum of 2 years. Early parole was not an option for anyone. They all lost their public office benefits. None of them can ever hold public office again.

The former cabinet members were all given heavy sentences and can never seek public office, as well, even if they live long enough after serving time. They also lost all benefits.

The United States became a military-controlled country for two years after David Holloway took command. The borders became secure. Immigration was put on permanent hold. The illegal immigrants were escorted out of the country. The remaining legal immigrants were given one year to pass an English test and were informed they needed to comply with all constitutional laws; if not, they would be deported immediately. All US citizens were fingerprinted. US companies were offered a healthy tax credit if they brought jobs back to America. All foreign aid had been put on hold indefinitely. The national debt had been cut 75% since Holloway had set foot on Capitol Hill. Nobody received any federal aid, unless drug screened and interviewed first. The country became self-dependent for all energy needs, thus drastically lowering consumer costs.

GREED DESTROYED WHAT OUR FOREFATHERS HAD BUILT

About the Author

Upon graduating from high school, I spent three years in Germany with the United States Air Force. After college, I spent my entire career selling and managing salespeople.

I spent a year, part time, under the direction of a Doctor of English from the University of Denver, learning the skills of writing. I attended a six month working seminar in Boulder, Colorado headed up by an experienced author and teacher.

I have traveled to four continents covering over thirty countries and have spent time exploring all 50 states. Articles on my travels have been published in a US newspaper and a European paper, as well. I currently reside in Florida.

Acknowledgement

I would like to thank everyone who has encouraged me to write. A special thanks to Terry Whalin who submitted my work to Morgan James Publishers. Also, I give thanks to Margo and Bethany and everyone else at Morgan James for their hard work. I am very grateful for the dedication, hard work and suggestions Paula Indriso has put into "Fatal Serum." Without her, "Fatal Serum" would not be on the shelf.

Printed in the USA
CPSIA information can be obtained
at www.ICGtesting.com
JSHW022326140824
68134JS00019B/1315